5150

BY DUNCAN MacLEOD

Published in the U.S.A. • Studio Squeeze Press

©2015 Duncan MacLeod. All rights reserved.

For information on the author you may contact him at
www.dunkablog.com or *@DuncanMac*

Cover and interior design by Wayne M. DeSelle / deselle.com

This book takes place in a real time and a real place. The people in the book are probably real, but then again, I was psychotic when I met them, so maybe they are not.
If you think you see yourself in here, you may be mistaken.
And if you thoroughly expected to be in here, maybe you need to take a closer look, because some people could be a mish-mash of a bunch of other people.

FOREWORD
By Brenda Knight

I wonder what the original architects of 237 Steiner Street, AKA "The Pink Palace," would think if they knew that this Pepto Bismol-shaded shack on stilts would become the Punk-rock version of Yaddo Artists Colony? One apartment, in particular, #3, seems to have fomented an unreasoning surplus of creativity with several award-winning authors, publishers, zinesters, musicians, filmmakers and even an odd couple whose patter was so outrageously entertaining, it has been sampled everywhere from Nirvana to NPR's This American Life in "Shut Up, Little Man: The Misadventures of Peter and Raymond."

Was it the ectoplasm?

This apartment #3, set in the low rent paradise of the Lower Haight, is also the setting of an early scene in Duncan MacLeod's singular novel, 5150. MacLeod gathers a motley cast of characters to solve a metaphysical mystery lurking beneath the cheap and profoundly hideous linoleum of a hippie witch's kitchen. Not unlike Lewis Carroll's Alice, the protagonist, Ethan, descends into a Looking Glass Land peopled by stranger-than-fiction San Franciscans. And then it really gets weird.

5150 evidences a bold new literary talent. MacLeod will have you laughing one minute and crying the next as you time-travel back with him to one of the city's grubbiest golden eras. MacLeod makes you care about the characters (even the nasty ones) as he pulls you into Ethan's vortex. 5150 is a portrait of a certain San Francisco's Lost Generation, captured brilliantly by Duncan MacLeod.

Author's Introduction

THE EXPERIENCE OF LOSING TOUCH *with reality and undergoing a psychotic break is perhaps the single most frightening thing that can happen to a human being short of a near-death encounter. Although I changed most of the names, the locations and the incidents described in this book are all based on a real events that occurred in my life in 1987. In 1986, I graduated from a prestigious prep school on the East Coast and went off to Columbia University to continue my upward trajectory towards fame, fortune and success. My brain had other plans for me.*

By the winter of 1986, I had come mildly unglued, fighting off depression and loneliness with alcohol, cigarettes and drugs. In a desperate attempt to hold on to my sense of self, I returned to the Bay Area to be close to my father and my beloved Aunt Jacqui. The arrogance of youth, a diet of pizza and beer, and a continued determination to "make it on my own" landed me in the Tenderloin, sharing a studio apartment with a beloved friend who was struggling himself with heroin. This set the stage for the ungluing that took place in June 1987.

To help the reader understand exactly what constitutes madness, I chose to tell the story in the first person present tense, intertwining actual events with my perception of the events themselves. Although I doubt I was able to float or hear the thoughts of others, for the moment, it was what I thought was happening. So even though this is technically a work of fiction, it is intended as a manual for understanding the thoughts, feelings and perceptions of the psychotic mind.

Young Ethan is actually young Duncan. It was only through the grace of God and the amazing capacity of the human body to heal itself that I was eventually able to return from madness to the place I am now, where I could write this book and share the psychotic experience with my readers. So thank you for attempting to understand the mentally ill. I met so many hundreds of young men and women who were struggling with the same racing thoughts, broken logic, fantastical and magical thinking, and sadly, very few ever returned from that place. A psychiatrist I met at the time said that the psychotic person is "drowning in the waters in which the mystic swims." It was an intensely mystical experience. The desire to return to that state is powerful, for when we are there, we no longer have to follow the rules of logic, or listen to the prevailing scientific method that permeates all of our lives.

I have never doubted that I was given a mission while in touch with the mystical realm of angels, to bring back a measure of understanding that might allow the loved ones of the mentally ill know that even in our madness, we are still human and capable of feeling love, sympathy, affection and understanding. Please read this book with this message in mind.

Los Angeles, Califronia ~ September 2010

515O

I hear the alarm ringing, but I don't get up. If I wait one whole minute, it will stop ringing, and I can stay here. There is a place called "home" and I am still looking for it. It is in my dreams, and the alarm is taking it away from me. I don't want to give up looking. Nor do I want to go looking for work. I have a great job in the dream. The alarm can't take that away from me.

All this week I've felt like there were tiny earthquakes in my bed. Just before I fall asleep, I feel the room shaking. Donny says it's just my heart beating. We live in a tiny apartment in the Tenderloin. We each took a walk-in closet as our room. Donny is over six feet, so his feet stick out of the closet when he sleeps. Donny looks like a gargoyle on a Gothic church. I love Donny. He is the most important person in my life. I wouldn't know what to wear, what to smoke, what drugs to do, none of it if I didn't know Donny. When we smoke pot we always get the giggles. I have a recording of us on pot, and all we do is laugh. We got kicked out for getting the cats high at our last house, and that's pretty much why we're living in the Tenderloin in this dingy studio.

The walls of the apartment are stained with age. The landlord could not blot out the grease and cigarette smoke with mere paint. Mildew creeps through the bone white in strange patterns that are starting to remind me of Tibetan sand paintings.

Eighteen-year-olds don't buy furniture. We just pile all our worldly possessions in heaps, which we sort through. The apartment is littered with heaps of clothing; tufts of fake zebra fur and black leather mark the different piles. Zebra fur is pants, leather is jackets. I don't have a job-hunting heap yet. I don't know what to wear to an interview, and I don't know where I want to work. I used to think I wanted to work in a gay bar for the rest of my life. I lied and said I was 21. Today I don't know what I want to do. I'm meeting Sue for coffee at the Café Flore in an hour, so I'd better get in the shower and find my job-hunting clothes somewhere in the heap of night-club clothes.

I love the smell of Aqua Net. My hair doesn't look good without a good, long spray of white Aqua Net, a crimp and a tease. I can't figure out how to put on makeup, so I usually just rely on my natural good looks to get me by. Donny knows how to put on makeup. Not me. I found my black suede creepers, so I'm ready to leave. Donny is still asleep. I can hear his snores from inside the closet.

The Stud closed last Friday. I worked there during the last six months before the evil transsexual owner of the building evicted the bar so she could open her own bar. The Stud had been there for 21 years, in an old building that once housed a church called The Universal Life Corral. The first time I went to the Stud I was 17 years old, last year. I used my fake ID that I bought in New York to get in. I remember being so nervous that my stomach hurt and I had to go to the bathroom, which wasn't very private.

They say the Stud was a really sleazy bar in its day, back in the dark ages, during and after Stonewall. But in the 1970s, it became known as the place where "the hippies dance with the punks." Now in the '80s it's just the coolest fucking place on Earth. Or it was, until last Friday. Now we're all supposed to go down there and help make the New Stud, two blocks away, into a great place. For NO PAY. We're just supposed to volunteer to strip and varnish the whole damn place, no questions asked. Just show up, work, go home, starve. They don't even buy us lunch. I can't live like that. And I know they won't let me work there if I don't do it.

If you work at the Stud, you're "family." Family helps each other out. Some of the creepier members of the family perv on you and tell you that they can get you fired because they know you're not 21, and they're going to tell someone. Family can get you pot and coke for a good price. But they don't have any heroin, never touch the stuff. You have to go to darker, seedier places to find heroin. Or so Donny tells me. I've never tried it.

*

If you sit under the wisteria at the Flore, you can totally get away with smoking pot. Sue and I are really stoned. An old man in OshKosh B'Gosh overalls and an engineer's hat shares a toke with us. He has the pot. The crags of his face are lined with a light dusting of dirt. He rides the rails. He tells me how I can catch a train to LA from the train yard in Oakland. Sue thinks it's not such a good idea. But there's a whole city down there I've never seen. I don't have any reason to stay here, do I? The Stud is closed, they want to enlist me as a slave laborer. How am I supposed to pay my rent in the meantime? Not only do they pay me under the table, it's also against the law for me to work there. So unemployment is out. Fuck it, I'm going to Hollywood.

The engineer says you got to go early if you want to hop a train. They run all day, but he always has better luck in the morning. You get off at West Oakland, go a few blocks east until you come to where the railroad tracks cross Peralta. And you wait. And when it comes, there are always empty boxcars.

Sue is older, more experienced, and very cool. She doesn't have any job ideas for me. But she's going to a séance at Wanda's house, do I wanna go? Yeah. Wanda lives just a few blocks away in the Lower Haight. It used to be an all-black neighborhood, but recently some punks moved in, and it's starting to change. Wanda lives in a pink stucco apartment building with aluminum windows, the only modern building on the block. Sue giggles as we enter Wanda's house. Wanda is sprawled out on the peach-colored sofa, watching the Prince Special on MTV. Wanda is a beautiful, buxom blond from West-by-God-Virginia who shrieks when we walk in.

"Suzie! Where did you find the fop? He's just a Little Lord Fauntleroy of Dickensian foppery on a wheeled stick!"

"This is Ethan. A new inductee to your coven!" Sue giggles

as she says "coven."

"Ethan! Oh, we're glad to have you. I'm hoping we can get to the bottom of my linoleum mystery."

I'm feeling bashful in spite of the fact that I immediately like Wanda. I've never met anyone as smart as Wanda before. She looks at me and says to Sue, "Where did you find him?"

Sue just snickers and says, "The Stud."

Wanda grows earnest. "Sue, you find so many valuable things down there at the Stud. It's just a treasure trove of gay fabulousness."

It turns out that the purpose of the séance is to find out why the bubble in Wanda's kitchen linoleum won't go away. Apparently, she's tried everything from nails to hot glue guns, and it just keeps coming up, a sure sign of a "haint." Wanda leaves me in the living room while she half flies, half walks into the bedroom and starts setting up for the séance. Kim follows her in to whisper secret stuff about me. While I'm waiting, I flip through an Aleister Crowley book on Wanda's coffee table called 777. The stuff in there doesn't make any sense at all to me, but it is definitely affecting my mind. The words are coming at me, like little men with arrows, attacking me. I'm not THAT stoned, this book is freaky shit. I'm starting to think that maybe it's casting a spell on me, so when I hear Wanda crow like a loon, I gladly put 777 down and run into the bedroom.

The séance starts. We turn off the overhead, light the candles, and put the tape recorder on. This reminds me of being eight years old and talking to ISIS on the Ouija board. Wanda calls forth the spirits of the North, South, East, and West winds. She brings sacred healing energy into the space. She then invites a spirit to make itself known. Wanda asks the spirit why she won't let her linoleum lie flat. Nothing. Then she asks the spirit to tell our fortunes. Nothing happens, the candle flickers. At the flicker, Wanda gasps. I realize that it's the little things, like the flicker of a candle or the slight tremor of a Ouija device, that mark the contact with the spirit world. Spirits are definitely in the room now.

I say, "I feel cold." Sue squeezes my hand and giggles reassuringly. Wanda shushes her. I feel unwell, like when you first come down with a cold. We break the circle, and the feeling subsides.

After the ceremony, we play the tape back. At highest volume, we can hear a faint voice on the tape, and he sounds really scary. He is roaring softly, like someone who is in pain on a distant hilltop. Wanda shudders and says she didn't know it was a man that was causing trouble in the kitchen. She says she had pictured an angry black woman. The voice is very faint. We can't make out much of what he's saying except that there is going to be a war, and that there will be blood. Then the tape starts to hiss like a snake. Suddenly, Wanda's voice comes through at top volume, scaring me so badly that I nearly pee my pants. Wanda can see I'm not feeling well, and she hugs me maternally to her. "It's okay, Ethan, it's over now."

I get up and go watch MTV. It was scary. Wanda comes out to see me on the couch.

"We're gonna have some champagne, do you want any?"

"Nah, I'm kinda beat."

"Well you just stay perched right there and cluck or squeak if you need anything at all."

Wanda glides gracefully into the kitchenette to find a bottle opener.

*

Donny is awake when I get home. He asks me if he can make a phone call to New Jersey to his parents. I say, "Go ahead, make as many calls as you want because I can't pay it anyway." His boyfriend is in Hawaii right now, so he calls him. They talk for four hours while I'm taking a nap.

When he gets off the phone, I call my mom in Vermont. She got a copy of my grade report from Columbia and saw all the Ds and Fs and she wanted to know if I was doing drugs. I say, "No, of course not because I don't do drugs." She doesn't believe me. Then I say that if she was working instead of finding God or Buddha or whatever on the commune in Vermont, then I would have had more time to pay attention to my studies instead of working until four in the morning at the Milk Bar.

She says, "Don't hand me that crap" and her voice makes that weird shrieking sound that makes my stomach hurt whenever I hear it. So I hang up. She calls back and says, "I'm ashamed of you." I say fine and hang up again. But then I call her back and she's crying. She says it's really important to her that I respect what she's doing because it's the most important thing in her life, and it should be really important to me too. I lie and say it's really important. Good. She's happier. It's time for the evening meditation, and she has to get off the phone.

"Bye."

Donny says, "What the fuck is her problem?" He has never met her, but he doesn't like her. He says, "She's an evil cunt."

I get mad and say, "No she's not." Then he gets out what's left of our little baggie of pot and packs the pipe. We smoke it down to the resin hits. I start to feel that earthquake feeling again, and now I'm not even asleep. Maybe I should lay off the pot. After this.

I get out a piece of paper and start drawing big, squiggly drawings. The pen never leaves the paper; I just make all the lines run into each other. I draw Donny and the spider in his ring and the Empire State Building with drugs coming out of the top of it, like a needle. I'm bored in San Francisco; I want to go back to New York. Then I remember the guy from the Café Flore. He was so cool. So I say to Donny that we should go to LA. Donny proclaims: "There's no way we can afford it."

I tell him that we can hop a train in Oakland, it's really easy and the guy told me how. Donny wants to go to LA, and hopping a freight train sounds cool, but he doesn't think it will work. "Oh my fucking God, yes it will," I scream. Donny looks at me like I'm crazy and shrugs. I say, "Let's go tomorrow." Then the giggles hit us really bad, and we eat all the bread because we don't have anything else. The resin gives me a headache.

I don't have much money, except my final pay from the Stud, which I am supposed to get tomorrow morning. That should be enough for a couple of weeks in LA, and we can worry about stuff when we get back, let's just go and have fun. It's starting to sound so good now, so we're psyched. It's dark out, and I want to go to the Underground and dance, but we're going to have to scam our way in because I'm flat broke, and Donny hasn't worked since he moved to San Francisco.

Let's do it. We put in an extra helping of Aqua Net, heat up the crimper, and the house fills with the bitter scent of sizzling hair. Donny has some kohl eye shadow that I want really bad. He puts some on me and says I have to learn how to do my own makeup. While he's putting it on, I try not to look in his eyes because it's embarrassing. The way he puts on my makeup feels really good, like I'm being pampered. I love the feeling of his fingers on my skin. Maybe I love him. But he looks like a gargoyle, and I want someone who looks like a jock. Then why am I wearing all this makeup and dressing like a skull dagger? It doesn't work, does it? Oh well. At least I'm cool.

Donny calls Lola, and she says she can help us scam our way in. He hangs up the phone and looks at me with a hunger in his eyes that I recognize all too well. It's dope fiend hunger.

"What?" I try to act all innocent.

"She was fucked up."

"How could you tell"?

"You just know." Donny wants some. Well, I have 30 dollars stashed somewhere and what the hell. I mean, I'm broke when it comes to food, but suddenly I have money for drugs. It's weird. And heroin? I'm afraid.

CHAPTER 2

When we get to the Underground, the door scene is really tight. We know a bartender there named Rory, so we ask if he's in there. The doorman says we have to leave an ID if we want to go talk to him. I don't think it's such a good plan. In New York, they'd just let us in because we were way cooler than the bridge and tunnel troglodytes who go to the big clubs. But this town is small, and they don't do that sort of thing. Then we see Lola, her olive green eyes pinned and fluttery. She has a stamp on her hand, and she says come here, and we go down Tehama Street and she spits so that the ink gets real wet and comes off her hand onto Donny's. I can tell she likes Donny better than me, or she would have done me first. Everyone likes Donny better because he's so cool. It doesn't work quite as well on my hand, but if we go to the back door, they'll never check. We just walk past the doorman, throw some attitude, and he half glances at the smears of black ink on our hand and lets us in. We're just another set of freaks to him. Downstairs there's dancing and lots of little goth kids, even younger than I am, who drove in from Burlingame in their parents' Buick Skylark. Lola sits us down and tells us that she can get us heroin if we pay her up front. Donny gets real excited, but I'm still afraid. He just pushes my shoulder and says, "C'mon, you've always wanted to try it," and now I want to. He knows what's cool.

I ask, "Can I get addicted from the first try?" and they both laugh.

We go back toward the apartment in Lola's car. She pulls over on O'Farrell Street and rings the phone doorbell. She disappears inside the building with our money for a really long time. When she comes out, she talks more slowly, and I'm pretty sure she did a little bump and so is Donny, but we don't say anything because that's just the way it works.

*

Back in our apartment there's no chairs, so we sit down on the piles of clothing. Lola goes into the kitchen and gets a spoon. We have a whole bunch of spoons but hardly any knives and only two forks. Donny lights a candle, and Lola puts a lump of tar, it looks like molasses, in the spoon. She heats it up with some water over the candle flame, making sure not to boil it.

"Why do you have to heat it up?"

"I don't know. It doesn't work if you don't cook it."

She says that if she goes first, then she won't shake, and she can hit me up. That's a lie, but I don't say anything. She puts a belt around her arm, and I turn away because I can't watch. Then Donny goes next. He gets a real serious look on his face, like I hardly ever see him, and when he lets the belt go, he exhales a long, slow sigh and turns to me and says he's glad it's so good for my first time. He's been beat real bad before, and, "This shit is really good." There isn't very much left in the spoon, but I won't need very much because it's my first time. I worry about overdosing. Before I'll use the needle, I say I need to bleach it. They both roll their eyes, but I go into the kitchen, and there's some bleach under the sink that was there when we moved in. I put some bleach in the glass and clean out the needle a few times, then I rinse it with water, drawing it up and squirting it out. When I'm done, the plunger won't move; it's too sticky. So Lola says, "Rub it on your ear, it will make it slide better." I don't believe her, but I take out the plunger and rub it against my ear. Sure enough, it moves okay after that. She says that earwax is a natural body lubricant, so it won't give me cotton fever. I've heard of cotton fever. It's a really bad headache that makes junkies bundle up in a knot and shake. You get it from the cotton you use to filter the heroin. Or that's what they say, anyway. I have to stop thinking about cotton fever. I wrap the belt around my arm. Lola starts touching my vein, and I can't watch, so I turn away.

I hardly feel it go in. When it's done, I don't notice anything. It's because I'm holding onto the belt really tightly, let go. So I let the belt go, and everything goes warm and fuzzy. My thoughts, which usually come at me real fast, come hardly at all. I feel like I'm on my journey home. I feel numb. Not just on my skin, but in my head too. I wish dying felt like this. Maybe it does. I try to stand up, but I fall right back down on the pile of clothes. Donny and Lola are just lying there, so what do I need to get up for? We talk softly under our breath about the universe. Lola thinks it's like a mirror. She says that whatever you hold up to it is what you see. I say it's like a tiny speck of dust floating down from a rooftop, heading toward a big barrel of rainwater. In a few million years, we'll all get real wet. Donny nods out and doesn't say anything. I say that the stars we see out there are just views of our own solar system at different times because time folds on top of itself, and we can see through it. Lola wrinkles her nose at me, like she isn't following me. It doesn't matter. I'm hungry. I don't know how long we've been sitting here, but I think I just woke up out of a nod. Lola doesn't have a lot of money, and so she offers to take us to the Grubstake. It's just a few blocks from here. It's an old diner in the shape of a railroad car. It's crowded with old trolls and hustlers. The yellow walls are stained with rust-colored grease. I can't really taste my burger, so I don't finish it. I usually eat all my food. I'm not hungry either, which is unusual for me. It's as if everything is being taken care of, and I don't need to worry about anything.

After the Grubstake, Lola drives us out to the beach to watch the sunrise. My nose is runny. The warm feeling is starting to wear off, and I'm tired. The ocean looks like a gray smear. The sun rises from behind us, so we hardly notice. The beach just warms from gray to brown. I am really cranky. I do my best to hide it from them because they both look really happy. I have to get my check from the Stud tomorrow. It's today, actually, and I haven't slept. I'll get it in the afternoon; we can ride the rails the next day. After what seems like an eternity, we finally drive back to the Tenderloin. I crawl into my closet and close the door. The earthquakes are really bad. I can hardly fall asleep, I'm shaking so hard. Donny is snoring.

*

I don't remember when I fall asleep, but when I get up, it's almost evening time. I have to run down the street to the Stud and get my check before the accountant leaves. I get there just as he's locking up. He shakes his head at me and goes in to get the envelope, muttering to himself softly under his breath. They pay me 30 dollars a shift. There's no bonus, like I was hoping. So I have 150 dollars to live on for the next three months while the Stud is closed. Well, let's see, rent is $375. How am I going to make 225 dollars in two weeks? And who's going to buy groceries? Not Donny. If I stay in town, I guess I'll be going to the soup kitchen on Waller Street. No problem. When I get home, Donny is up and he's hungry. I go to the corner and buy broccoli and an onion and a can of broth. I make soup from it. It tastes shitty. It smells like the garbage chute. I don't know how to make fucking soup.

I put the rest of the soup in the refrigerator. Donny wants fried chicken, so I go to the KFC on the corner and consider the cost of a bucket versus a box. Maybe I can put some of the chicken in the soup to make it taste better.

At the KFC an old lady sits in one of the brown, plastic chairs, fingering a bruise on her leg. Her hair is matted, her face speckled with mud, and she laughs and sings to herself. She says my name, Ethan. How odd. As her vocal chords hum and create laughter, I can hear some sort of message masked under the noise. She is telling me that the chicken is poisoned. I get out of line and thank her. I go to the Banh Mi store and get two chicken buns. Donny doesn't like them, but it's better than poison, I explain. Donny ignores my revelation about the poison chicken. He eats the bun with a disgruntled look on his face. He wrinkles his nose every so often, the salty flavor disagrees with him. Later I hear him throwing up in the bathroom. Maybe there was no way to avoid the poison chicken, like the oracle at Delphi. That woman was an oracle! Or maybe he's just dope sick.

*

Tonight I go for a walk in the Tenderloin. There are brown stains all over the sidewalks. Where do they come from? Some of them are old chewing gum. They look like polka dots. Wait, are they arranged in a pattern? I don't want to miss anything. Some of them are covered with cardboard. Old bums lie on the cardboard, drinking Cisco from a brown bag, leaned up against the corner liquor store. One piece of cardboard says "Lux" on it. Lux means light, and so I follow the light. A dog runs out of a doorway and growls at me. I turn toward him, and he wags his tail. I reach down and pet the dog. He has a wound in his neck. The owner appears menacingly in the doorway and kicks the dog, nearly clipping my face. I just keep walking.

Ghostly women haunt the hallways whose doors open out onto the street. Nice bag of water, wanna nice bag of water? Late night, satellite. Late night, satellite. Hey Ethan! I keep hearing my name.

The Tenderloin is creepy, so I head toward Union Square. The crowds of tourists are dwindling. A cable car passes me on Powell Street, and the conductor shouts Ethan. Why do I keep hearing my name? Is somebody trying to reach me? Blondie's Pizza is closing, and they drag the trash can out front. There is a whole pizza on top. I share the pizza with an old man who was waiting for it. The pepperoni is still warm, the grease puddle in the middle of each slice runs down the cheese and onto my chin. Oh good, they threw away some napkins too.

CHAPTER 3

When I get home Donny is gone. I can't sleep, so I stay up watching the broken black-and-white television. There's nothing on, just an old Pat Boone musical and an advertisement for phone sex. The television sputters and threatens to burn out. I turn it off. It smells like burning dust. Outside the window I see an old chair in front of the flower shop. I go out and grab it. It is damp, but it works. Good, now we have a chair. When I get it upstairs, I see that it has a cracked leg. I sit on it carefully, and it doesn't break. Good.

Tomorrow we're going to LA on the freight train. I pack my backpack with a change of clothes and the wool American flag to use as a blanket.

Food... I check the fridge to see if the soup is still there. I lift the pot lid, and the unmistakable stench of bad broccoli knocks me over like a sucker punch. I put the lid back on the pot as quickly as I can. Better leave it. I go back to Banh Mi and get a chicken sandwich for myself. Donny can pick what he wants later.

At about 6 a.m. Donny comes home. He smells like sex. He says he fucked some guy for 50 dollars. Great, now he can get his own chicken sandwich from KFC.

I remind Donny that we're catching the train to LA tomorrow. He rolls his eyes. I want him to be as excited as I am about it, but he just isn't. I set the alarm clock for noon. I want to get an early start.

*

The alarm annoys me when it goes off. I get up and Donny says, "What the fuck was that?" Then I brush my teeth and wipe the sleep out of my eyes. Donny takes a bit longer to get ready; he puts his makeup on, which I think might be a bad idea if we run into real hobos, but I don't say anything. On the way to BART, we stop at Burger King for our meal. We get an extra chicken sandwich for later, on the train.

The BART train lets us off in West Oakland, by the post office. It's a few blocks to the train yard. When we get there we don't see any trains. There's an old wall-eyed black man digging a hole in between some tracks, and he shows us which tracks are heading south. We wait in a ditch by the tracks. It's late afternoon and it's pretty hot out. Donny's makeup starts running down his face. After about two hours, Donny says we should ask someone when the train is coming. I find the wall-eyed man again, and he says, "The LA train don't come until 'round about nine o'clock. The morning train's the one to catch, boys. Gotta get up real early." Great. It's only five-thirty, and we have some time to kill. We walk around West Oakland, which is not a pretty place. Many of the buildings are dilapidated and condemned. Red-rimmed eyes peer out from behind tattered curtains as we walk past. The hair parlor smells like hot combs and no-lye relaxer.

We find the Amtrak station, where we sit and watch the clock. The station is very old, probably a hundred years old. The bathroom smells like crack and baby sick. They sell snacks, and Donny loads up on corn chips and soda pop so we don't go hungry or thirsty on the way down. The announcer comes over the loudspeaker and says my name. I wander away to try and find out why they paged me. The lady at the counter looks at me like I'm crazy. How would anyone know I was here, anyway? Who cares about me enough to page me at the train station? Maybe it's Sue. I get on the phone and call her. She says no, but what am I doing at the train station? I explain about riding the rails and she giggles. Why didn't I invite her? "You wanna come?" I ask, and she says no. I see Donny standing by the luggage looking around for me, so I gotta go, and I get off and go see Donny. He says what the fuck am I doing leaving the luggage and I say someone paged me, and he says no they didn't. Donny brought a copy of Naked Lunch, which he reads while we wait. I don't have anything to read, but there's a newspaper. When I try to read it, my concentration just isn't there. Maybe it's all the excitement about leaving for LA. I can't even tell what the paper is saying. The headlines might as well be written in Sanskrit. I just don't understand what they're trying to say. This worries me a little because I used to be really smart. Oh well.

Time crawls by really slowly. Around eight-thirty we head back to our ditch. It's foggy out, and the grass is covered in dew, and we get wet lying there, waiting for the train.

*

The train is late. I don't know what time it is, but we must have waited here another couple of hours. Then we hear the whistle. It's the train! I can see the light. It is moving at a slow crawl. Donny has nodded off, so I push him, and we both stand on our feet, holding our luggage, ready to leap aboard. Trains create optical illusions as they move toward an object. They appear to be moving very slowly when they are at a distance, when, in fact, they are going fast. That's why so many trucks get creamed trying to run the train at a crossing. I discover this as the train approaches us. The train is going about 40 miles an hour. After the engine passes us, we both start running alongside the train, but it's way too fast. The empty boxcars rattle past us, and we can't get on. I trip in the ditch and land in a putrid mud puddle. Donny stops to help me up, and the train is gone. I start laughing, but Donny doesn't think it's so funny. I can't stop laughing. I say, "Let's wait here and catch the morning train," but Donny says, "No fucking way." He starts walking back to BART. I don't want to sleep alone in a ditch in West Oakland, so I follow him. It's almost midnight when we get to BART, and we're lucky to catch the last train back into the city. Donny won't even look at me, and I can't stop laughing, which makes things worse. My ears pop in the tunnel under the bay. I think about what if the train gets stuck in here during an earthquake, and the tube bursts and fills with water and we drown. I always think that when I'm in the Transbay tunnel. I'll bet everybody does.

CHAPTER 4

I wake up with a jolt. Was there an earthquake? I hear a ringing in my ear now. It sounds like the public address system at my elementary school. I'm waiting for the omnipotent principal to give me instructions. It goes away. What is that noise trying to tell me? It must mean something.

There's a phone bill in the mailbox. I want to pay it. There's about two hundred dollars in calls to Hawaii. How am I going to pay it? I told Donny I wouldn't, so why am I changing my mind? Fuck it; I won't pay the phone company. The phone still works.

I lie down on the floor and look at the ceiling. I'm seeing patterns. Weird. Maybe it's an acid flashback. Donny says he always gets them when he's tired. But I'm not tired. I feel really awake, in fact.

Suddenly, I get an idea. It's about photography. David Hockney used to take multiple Polaroids of swimming pools and reassemble them like a jigsaw puzzle and then paint them. I want to do photographs like that and make collages. The collages will be taken in a circle, instead of a square, and the result will be a mandala. It's going to be so beautiful. I'll color-xerox them and sell them. That's how I'll make money. I need a camera. I have about 65 dollars left; that should be enough for a camera. I'm really excited now. I've never been artistically inspired like this. I usually feel like I can't draw or paint or even take pictures, but this is a gimmick. It's gonna really sell. I think that's what the ringing sound in my ears meant. They sell Polaroids at Walgreens. But let's think about this. I don't want the white borders on my photographs. I want the picture to go right to the edge of the paper. And the last time I tried to cut a Polaroid, it bled all over the place with some hideous toxic goo. So no Polaroids. I need an Instamatic camera. This is going to be great! I'll do portraits. They'll be so beautiful, even the President will want one. I'll make a fortune. This is a really great idea. I've got a plan for the tripod I'll use too. I mount the camera on a wheel and rotate the reel a notch and take a picture and then rotate it again. And the camera will rotate twice, once near the center of the axis and once out on the edge of the giant wheel. I need a bicycle wheel or something to mount the camera on. I'll do my first few by hand; they should work okay. The giant wheel - that's Earth too, and life on this planet, karma, it all is starting to make a lot of sense now. I understand why Mom lives on a Buddhist commune now.

Outside, the streets sound like a washing machine on spin cycle. I want to get some portraits made before the idea is gone. The clerk at Walgreens is too slow. "No, I don't want a disposable camera, I want a permanent one, yes that one, and some indoor film. Indoor. Yeah, that's it. Thank you." I forget my change. I don't care.

Back at home, Donny is finally up. He is sitting in the kitchen, drinking a cup of coffee. "Hold it right there. Can I take your portrait?"

He shrugs. "What are you doing, Eeth? Why is the camera

upside down?"

"Hold still! It's a cool idea I had. Okay, there."

I want my photos developed in an hour. The Vietnamese coffee shop has a xerox shop and a one-hour film processor. I can have a cup of coffee while I wait. Every time the owner says something loud to his little girl in the back, I think he's calling my name. I come to the counter to get the photos, and he says not yet. Why did he call my name? Weird. This is really starting to irritate me. I go home after my cup of coffee and get Donny. He can tell me when they call my name. Donny doesn't want to go. I drag him with me. He rolls his eyes.

The photos are ready. I get a piece of paper from the owner. Donny doesn't get it. I show him. See, I'm assembling it. It isn't really working too well. But see, that's the idea. Donny shrugs. He wants a job. I tell him he has to get a job at a one-hour processing place so I can get it done for free. He looks at me in an odd way and asks me if I'm all right. "Fine, fuck you!" I scream it at him. I run as fast as I can away from him, crying. How am I going to do my art? I walk down Eighth Street to the new Stud location. Lola pulls up in her car with a friend.

"How you doing?"

"Great, look at my art! I got this great new idea, and I'm going to make a million dollars."

She scrutinizes it and says "great." She asks me if I'm okay.

"Yeah, of course. I'm on my way to the Stud to show them, gotta run. Bye."

The Stud. They're all there, volunteering. I show Brian Egg

my art project. All he asks is where have I been? I won't have a job if I don't start showing up to help out with the move. He just doesn't get it. None of them get it. Fuck them all. I run out of there. They don't understand me. They still think I'm 21, not 19. They don't really know me. Brian Egg runs out after me and calls my name. He waves me over, and I approach him. He has the longest hair I've ever seen. He is a genuine hippy fag. There aren't too many of them left now, it's the eighties and they all bought cars.

"Let me see that again." He points to my beautiful mandala.

"It's a mandala of Donny."

He takes it out of my hands and stares at it. He nods his approval and hands it back to me.

"Do you see the world like that?" He reaches into his pocket and takes out a packet of Zig-Zags while he waits for my response.

"I guess so."

"It's fractured."

He wields a little baggie full of green bud [right here in the middle of the sidewalk!] and pours some pot out of it into the paper.

"Brian, what if someone sees you?"

"I'm invisible."

"How?"

"Stand a little closer, you'll be invisible too." He pulls me a little closer to him. He rolls the joint adeptly, generously. It's beautiful. He lights it and takes a long, cross-eyed toke before handing it to me. It's so strong I cough, and my eyes immediately get that smoky haze around the edges.

"That's some shit."

"It's not SHIT!!" Brian is going off, like he always does. "I am plucked! Plucked you hear me!"

I back away from him. He is scary. But I am not afraid of him. He reminds me of my mother. Donny says we look related. "What are you plucked about?"

"You come around here while we're all mopping the floors and making this place," he gestures wildly with his hand and pauses. "...This place, we're making this place BEAUTIFUL. Beautiful, and you're just sitting around taking pictures." I don't think he gets how important this all is.

"Brian, I gotta go."

"Go. Just go. We're all working our ASSES off here, but just go."

*

Sue understands me. I bet she's home. She doesn't work right now. I have a lot of energy. I walk to the Castro to find her. She's at the Café Flore. I sit down and laugh with her. I tell her about Brian, and she says that he's always plucked. She says he's always madder than a wet hen too. I show her my art project, and she says she has some good paper that we could use to mount it so it doesn't get all bent up. I knew she would understand. We giggle and run to her house to smoke some of Dennis Peron's weed that she just scored. I sit in a weird bubble after I have the pot. There's a hollow crashing sound in my ears, like when you listen for the waves in a seashell. I start thinking about pot and why it's illegal. I don't think it should be. Neither does Sue, and neither does Dennis. Dennis is a crusader for the pot cause. I want to help him. I'm going to the library tomorrow to do some research. Donny calls and talks to Sue for a while before she hands the phone to me. He says where did I go. He's sorry. He's not sure what he did, but he's sorry anyway. I say I'm sorry too and we'll talk. He asks me to hand the phone back to Sue. She talks real quiet so I can't hear. She puts the phone down and asks me if I've been eating too much pizza. Why? Well, she says, pizza has flour and tomatoes, which are really bad for your brain. My brain is fine, never been better. So I must not be eating too much pizza, what a weird question! Sue just chuckles, and we fire up another joint.

I tell Sue about the phone bill. She looks concerned. She tells me that I shouldn't mess with the phone company like that, because they're really important. She's right. She says they can help me. Call them right now. So I do. This is such a good thing.

The lady I talk to is really nice. She says that Pacific Bell is really interested in keeping its customers. We set up a payment schedule, which is impossible, given that I don't have any income. She says that will cover my local calls, but she needs to transfer me to AT&T to deal with the rest of it. AT&T, AT&T, why does the name seem so important to me? I write it on a piece of paper. They have me on interminable hold. I get it! Isn't there a finance company called ITT? Are they related? I bet they are. And if you look at this carefully, it all makes sense. ITT makes sense. I know where ITT is ATT. I've solved the puzzle; I know where it's at. What does it mean to know where itt's att? I've never been on hold for this long. They must know I'm working out the puzzle.

Without warning, my entire life starts making glorious sense. It starts with my grandmother's maiden name - Stein. Wasn't Einstein number one (like ein in German)? And if I figure out this giant puzzle, doesn't that make me Stein number two? I'm Vaistein. I am the next genius. At just that moment that I make sense of my life, the AT&T customer service lady comes on the line. She is part of the most powerful company in the world. She knows I was figuring out the puzzle. She asks me how she can help me. I tell her that I know where itt's att. Oh, I see. What's my name? Vaistein, I tell her. Can you spell it? I-T-T I say. She says, "I don't think I can help you,;let me transfer you to a supervisor." Super Visor. This is the person who sees above her, who is more powerful. I won. I won the contest to figure ITT out. The Super Visor is going to tell me what I won. Sue is watching me from the kitchen. I can tell she's excited that I just figured itt out. Her smile says it all. I finally figured it out, and now I can be an adult. I don't have to work like a dog anymore. I can get a job with the most powerful company on Earth. When the supervisor comes on the line, I ask her for a job. Silence. I tell her I figured out where itt is att. "Okay, sir." She is laughing because she is so happy that I figured itt out. Maybe I'm missing outt. What would outt be? One Universal Telephone and Telegraph? I ask her if there's a subsidiary by that name. She says she will transfer me there. The phone starts beeping in my ear. It's a message. I wish I knew Morse code. But now I don't need it anymore. I can tell what the phone is saying. I've never heard like this before, it's part of my new power. It's asking me to choose a profession. Oh great, I got the job. I press the keypad to spell out the job. 3 (f) - 4 (i) - 5 (l) - 6 (m) - 6 (m) - 2 (a) - 5 (k) - 3 (e) - 7 (r). I want to make movies. I wait for a confirmation. The tone changes, and then the line goes silent. I guess that's it. Thatt's Itt. I'll wait and hear from them later. Wait! They don't have my address. Oh, yes they do, the Pacific Bell lady gave it to them. The bell of peace. Maybe that's something too, but I don't think it matters as much as where itt's att. I hang up. I make a mental note to work on the Liberty Bell-Pacific Bell connection when I have some time.

Sue looks at me and asks what the heck was going on. I tell her I figured out the puzzle. She says it's because I have Mercury in Aquarius. She knew all along.

CHAPTER 5

I don't remember how I got here. I'm at home. I have on my snowman pants and a T-shirt. I don't remember putting them on. Who put me here? Did Sue drive me here in the middle of the night? Did the phone company teleport me here? Where's Donny? I need to tell him about the puzzle and give him the message. I need him to take photos. The phone rings. It's AT&T. When I pick it up, there's a loud sound on the other end. It's a message. Another message from the phone company. They want me to press in my identification. I don't know who I am or who I want to be. I want to work for the phone company. I won't have to worry anymore, because I finally figured out where itt's att. I'll have a salary, and I'll get to go to Europe.

Or maybe I won't. I'm worried. There's no response at the phone company. I call the operator, and it says all circuits are busy, try again later. I keep trying, and it just keeps saying that. Now there's no dial tone. It's the worst, I fear. Aliens are coming. I have to hurry and pack my bags. What do I need? I need my camera, so I can take pictures. I need an identification of some kind, that's what the phone company asked me for. I don't want my driver's license. I burn it on the stove. Where's Donny? I want him to come. I love Donny. But he won't be Donny in the next place, where the aliens are taking me. I don't care any more. I feel Ethan slipping away. He is going away, far away. Who am I now? I have to go to the library to find out.

The gate slams behind me with a bang. It's too late, I don't have my keys. I can't go home. Donny's gone. The street is filled with people. None of them know. They just walk around with blank stares on their faces. They have no idea that aliens are coming. I resist the urge to tell them. If everyone knows, then there won't be room on the ship. I burnt my old ID; I need a new one. The library is right across the street. I run in and up the cold marble steps. I can see the X-rays as I walk through the book detector. There are spies here. The librarian asks if they can help me. They might be a spy from the phone company, and I don't want them to know that I lost my identity. So I just say "no." Like a bucket on a pulley, I am dragged up the stairs to the card catalog. I open the drawer that says STA-STE. I'm a Stein. There I am. It's Gertrude Stein. Her ISBN number: that should do. I yank the card out of the drawer, and secret it away in the camera case. No one saw me do it. Good, the phone company will never know the difference. My snowman pants don't have any pockets. Not the most sensible choice for an alien abduction, where I think pockets would come in handy. Oh well. Now I know who I am. I'm Gertrude Stein. I feel her wash over me. I feel old and uncomfortable. My back hunches a bit. My legs feel heavy. I think I should have chosen someone a bit younger. I hobble out of the library and down the steps.

The sun is much brighter than usual. The whole city is bathed in a yellow hazy glow. It must be the effects of the ship breaking through the earth's atmosphere. I don't know where the ship is, or where to find it. Maybe the aliens don't want me. There are messages from the aliens everywhere. I look at the graffiti on the concrete wall behind the library. Yes, there they are. I can't quite make it out. It looks like a Star of David inside of a circle. They communicate in symbols. Good, I can read them. It says, "Welcome." They're talking about me. There's more. They promise to take me up. I follow the trail of graffiti down the street. There are arrows, some of them hidden inside words. The arrows take me down Hyde to Market Street. The market. The great, big market. The arrows have stopped appearing. Where should I go now? I have to go say goodbye to Brian Egg at the Stud. I'm going up in the ship. AT&T told them to come for me because I figured out where itt's att. The Stud feels really far away. I'm Gertrude, and I'm too old to walk. I have to, though. Like magic, I have more energy. I feel really light. That must be Ethan, helping me out. I guess he's in here too. I walk down Eighth to the Stud. The whole crew is in there again, this time they are sitting around and talking instead of working. They see me and ask me to come over. "Ethan, Ethan." Wait, I'm not Ethan anymore. They can't see me, they'll ruin it, they'll blow my cover and the aliens won't take me. I run out of there without saying a word. Brian runs out and calls my name. I run so fast he can't see me. I'm invisible now, too.

I haven't stopped running for ten minutes. I'm at Sixth Street. 6. I feel good about 6. I walk up Sixth toward Market. People walk right past me and don't see me. I look into their eyes, and they don't see me. I am invisible. Just one more gift from the phone company. I am Gertrude Stein, I'm invisible, and I am about to be the guest of honor on the mother ship. Market Street. The electric bus comes off the rail. I did that. With my mind. The bus driver gets out and curses. I giggle. He can't see me. Where do people go when they are about to be abducted? I need to go to the highest point in San Francisco and wait. I look up. At the top of Nob Hill there's a tower. There, at the top of the Mark. The Mark, of course, it's like a treasure map, X Marks the spot. How come I'm the only one that figured this out? Or did everyone else figure it out and I'm just a slow learner. Where else would Gertrude Stein go if she were in San Francisco? The Mark. Jones Street is the steepest street I've ever climbed. It's not easy if you want to be abducted. After a few minutes, instead of being winded, I start floating. Now I can fly. I float up the hill, my feet barely touching the ground. The wind is carrying me up the hill like the red balloon floating over Paris. I am invisible and I can fly. At the crest of the hill, the cable car crawls by, filled with hundreds of tourists, completely unaware of what is going on. They can't see the difference in the light, and they can't see me either. I wonder if I can walk through walls now too? I'll try. I go into the Mark Hopkins. I don't have to touch the revolving door, it just moves. I am walking through walls. In the lobby, there's a bank of elevators. Without pushing a button, the elevator opens. I step in. Nothing happens for a minute, then the doors close. The phone company is taking me where I need to be. When the elevator doors open, a man is standing there. He's wearing a painter's cap and overalls. He can't see me. I walk past him. There's an open door. As I head toward the open door, the man in the painter pants suddenly yells. "Hey where are you going"?!! I guess my cloak of invisibility wore off. Shit. I go into the room and slam the door behind me. There are no carpets on the floor, no furniture, and the walls are wet with paint. So this is where Gertrude Stein is supposed to wait for the aliens. Some place. There are voices outside the door. They are banging on the door. Gertrude isn't safe anymore.

CHAPTER 6

I need to get rid of Gertrude. I don't have an ID card for anyone else. I'll just have to take my chances. I go into the bathroom and lock the door. The voices are getting louder. I turn on the bath. The water is cold. It gets hotter. I take off my snowman pants and t-shirt and climb into the tub. Gertrude begins washing off. I can feel the old wrinkled skin slipping off of me and into the bath water. I pull the drain plug and down she goes. The new identity, the one I didn't choose, is starting to take me over. Andy Warhol, who just died, is making an appearance now. He's in me. He hisses like a snake. There are voices in the room, just outside the bathroom door. They know I'm in here. Well, what am I waiting for? Isn't this why I came here? They're here. I guess I'm scared to leave Earth. I step out of the bathtub just as they break down the bathroom door. I am naked.

"Welcome," I say. I am expecting a warm reception. But something's wrong, terribly wrong. They are dressed like two policemen. I didn't realize that fascism exists in outer space as well.

They throw me to the ground and recite a long poem in blank verse. My right to remain silent is sacred. When aliens abduct you, they let you know in secret signs like this. They are visitors from another planet. "You don't have to hold me down, I'll go willingly," I say.

"Shut up." One of the visitors pushes my head into the hard

floor. There is no carpet, and bits of old carpet glue stick to my face. This is not the reception I was expecting at all. This sucks. I say so. I feel the clink of alien metal handcuffs around my wrists. They hurt. The left one is tighter than the right. Someone picks me up by the handcuffs, which really wrenches my shoulder. I thought I was going somewhere where there would be no more pain. I guess I was sadly mistaken. Now I really don't want to go. I say, "Fuck you." That was a mistake. Here I'm supposed to be grateful that they're getting me off of this godforsaken shit hole of a planet, and I'm insulting them. One of them hits me and says, "Shut up."

All these years I thought those old science fiction films that featured evil aliens were just xenophobic, pessimistic portrayals of man's innermost fears of the beyond. Maybe I was wrong. These aliens totally suck.

"What's your name," they ask me. I was prepared to tell them, but now I don't want to. I want to get lost. Harlow. Andy Harlow. That should confuse them. The uglier, wall-eyed one writes it down in his notebook.

The one that wrenches my arm is actually pretty handsome. "Put your clothes on!" he yells at me. I start laughing. I have handcuffs on. "How can I put my clothes on with handcuffs on?" The hot looking one lets me go for a second to grab my snowman pants for me. I take advantage of the moment to make a break for the door. No luck. Wall-eye stands in the doorway and keeps writing. "Where do you think you're going?"

"I don't know, I hoped you would tell me."

"Very funny." The hot one puts my pants on for me. His face is right by my dick and I begin to get a boner. He snarls and punches me in the gut and calls me faggot. So much for hot fascist alien fantasies. They hate faggots in outer space, too. I start to experience the weightless feeling again. I start to float away. Ugly asks mean hot alien how I am doing that. I giggle, because I am sure I stole the secret powers from them. They drag me like a helium balloon down the hallway to the elevator. My head hits the doorway on the way into the elevator, and I crash to the floor in a heap.

"That's the weirdest fucking thing I've ever seen," says ugly. They use curse words in outer space, do I really want to go? In the elevator, the looser handcuff slips off my hand. Why do I feel compelled to show them? I hope that maybe they'll treat me more gently if I show them. It doesn't work. Hottie grabs my face and squeezes it so I must look like a fish. "Stop fucking around," he tells me.

"I haven't fucked either of you yet." That was not the right thing to say. He bashes my head against the elevator wall just as the doors open. A gaggle of Nancy Reagan women gasp in horror as I am led past them. They look like a museum. They aren't human. I can see by their hair and jewelry that they aren't from here. They touch their pearls and whisper among themselves. They haven't seen a human like me before. They completely took over the Mark Hopkins Hotel. They draped a banner over the entryway; I can't quite make out what it says. Is it for me? Why are they so curious? Haven't they seen the cable car filled with tourists going by outside? What makes me so unique that all the alien Republican women are staring at me? Is it my hair? Is it my snowman pants? It's because I'm a fag. They haven't seen a fag before. I wave with my cuff-less hand, and Ugly grabs my wrists and clamps the cuff back on much tighter. It hurts now. We're outside in that strange alien haze, and there's a an alien transport in the circular driveway. It looks like a cross between an RV and an armored truck.

As they throw me into the transport, cutie pie with the fists says, "Have a nice trip." I guess they have to screen out potential troublemakers for the Intergalactic voyage. Apparently I passed. I almost blew it when I used their powers to float, but they didn't seem to know how I did it. And waving at the Republican aliens was a really bad idea, too. Odd. The truck is lined with galvanized metal. The kind with little cross hatches. I press my hand against it, and when I lift it away, there is writing on my hand. It's from Wanda. She is saying she'll see me on the other side. I guess the floor is a touch sensitive writing pad. I write a goodbye message to Wanda, and she writes me back not to tell people everything I know right away. Okay, Wanda.

After I get done writing on the floor, the truck takes off. I fall off my knees and roll into something soft behind me. The whole truck feels like it's made of the hardest metal alloy in the universe, and here is something soft. I turn around, and it's an old man. Or maybe he's one of them. How can I tell? He is wall-eyed, just like the ugly alien. He must be an alien too. I ask him if he's an alien. "You can't do it like that," he says, "You gotta laugh more." He starts to wheeze and chuckle. "See? Then they'll let you go." I am not certain I know what he's talking about. There is a tiny slit in the side of the truck, and light comes pouring in, in a camera obscura effect. It's too intense to be a mere camera obscura. They're feeding me information through light. I put my face in the light and absorb the knowledge. "What do you know?" he asks. I shrug.

"I know the Empire State Building is a hypodermic needle."

"Now you're getting it," he says.

Maybe I shouldn't have told him. That's one of the more important things that I knew, and Wanda says not to tell. I thought intergalactic voyages would be somewhat more luxurious than this. I feel like I accidentally took Aeroflot instead of Pan Am. There aren't even any seat belts. Some aliens these turned out to be. The old man laughs a great deal. He seems amused by me. Who is he? He tells me not to tell them my true name until afterwards. I thank him. He is pretty nice. Then his face turns very cruel and he starts shouting epithets at me. He calls me a cranny coon meister. What is he saying? I'll bet he's doing it as a rehearsal for his reception speech on the new planet. Judging by the general disposition of the aliens I met so far, he's being pretty polite. They must be Klingon. That's the only explanation I can think of. I ask him if that's true and he calls me a cocksucker freak. Jesus Christ! They have homophobes in all walks of life, but why are they transporting them to the new planet? How un-evolved. This is going to be one long trip.

But I guess I spoke too soon. The voyage is so short; it's

already over. I think I absorbed all the knowledge that was in the light, the in-flight movie, if you will. I don't feel like I know much more than before, except that Intergalactic travel is rather uncomfortable. The transport is in a holding bay. The door clangs open, and ugly grabs me gruffly. He pushes me out of the truck. "Harlow!" He shouts at me. I am glad he doesn't know who I really am. Am I glad? I'm really far from home now. Mistaken Identity. I told them a lie. I have a bad feeling. What if my real self was the key to getting in to the new planet? But who am I? I thought I was Andy Warhol when they got me. But now I'm starting to feel like Ethan again. I don't know who I am anymore. That's what the light in the space craft was doing. It was erasing my old self. It occurs to me that maybe I didn't get abducted, maybe I died. Maybe this is heaven. It doesn't look very nice. The walls are grimy yellow, there are fluorescent lights everywhere. It must be purgatory. Another alien dressed in dark blue comes out of the clear glass doors and they all have a pow-wow. "No ID, says his name's Harlow." The new alien comes over to me, and looks me up and down.

"You gotta name, boy?"

"Yessir. Ethan Lloyd."

"Great. How you spell that?"

"E-T-H-A-N-L-L-O-Y-D"

"Frisk em and put em in holding."

The cute one starts pinching me really hard. It hurts. This is an alien frisking, like one of those probes, only more painful. When he grabs my crotch, I scream out "don't castrate me!" This is not well received.

"Fucking shut up."

He pinches my balls really hard and snickers to himself. I don't like these aliens. They're worse than everything I ever read about alien abduction. They're too masculine. Why aren't there any women aliens? After pinching my ass, my cock and balls, my legs and my tits, he hands me a dollar bill. "Here, you're gonna need this." Where did he get it from? It has a portrait of George Washington on the front. Is this my new ID card? It looks like a dollar bill, but he told me I was going to need it. Why would I need American money in outer space? It must be something special. It's a message. They want me to be a leader. I get to be president now.

I am not so sure I'm ready to be president. I don't dare turn down an offer from the aliens from the phone company. If that's what they want, then that's what they'll get. I always have found that honesty is the best policy. "Sir, I'm not ready to be president."

"NO, you're not."

"Good, I'll wait."

"Yep, you'll wait." He pushes me rather gruffly up a grimy concrete ramp. It seems odd to see so earthy a material as concrete in an alien setting. I stoop low to check it. It's alien concrete. The cracks move like snakes. It looks like it's breathing. I reach down to touch it.

"Keep your ass moving!"

It's so easy to upset these aliens. They don't want me to know anything about the planet. I'm pretty sure that once I get past this docking bay, I'll be able to get a good wide view of the new planet. There are an awful lot of hallways in this terminal. They are lit by lights which use the same technology as our fluorescent lights, but they feel different. They make my skin glow bright green. I feel like cattle, the way this fierce alien in a cop suit keeps prodding me and pushing me forward. Why doesn't he just let me take in the new alien environment for a minute? I turn to ask him, but the look on his face is so menacing that instead I start to panic. What led me to believe that this was a good thing? Alien abduction, probes, missing children on milk cartons, and now it's some kind of honor to be here. Based on my treatment from the welcoming committee, which falls quite a bit short of the lei committee in Hawaii, I can guess that I'm in for a pretty shitty time here on whatever the fuck planet this is. Now I'm not enjoying myself. I look back on my treatment from the moment I made contact with the aliens. The honeymoon is definitely over. Faggot, huh? I'll show them a pissed off angry faggot, if they want it. I whip around toward the alien behind me, but he seems to have known what I was thinking. Before I even know what is happening, he has his boot on my head, grinding my teeth into the snakey shit brown alien floor. I have a really good view of the floor now. I am studying it, ignoring the boot and the pain that I feel. The floor is definitely made of a living material. It grows and swells, and the trails that run through it carry electrical signals, like some sort of intricate circuit. I let some drool escape from my mouth. When it lands on the concrete, it turns red, the color of blood. I am bound and determined to short-circuit this machinery at the first chance I get.

There are voices now, and I can see the reflection of a door opening in the pool of blood red spittle I left on the floor.

"Ease off of him, Jack."

"Mother fucker was about to head butt me."

"I don't think you have anything to worry about. He's not very strong. Look at his arms."

It's true. I have spindly arms. I'm sort of fat, but my arms are like broomsticks. They are useless arms, part of my whole useless body. My legs are a little more powerful, but I can't kick anyone with my arms cuffed behind my back anyway. I'd lose my balance. The gentler, kinder fascist alien lifts me by my cuffs and drags me to my feet.

"Put him in A-4."

The boot stomper drags me toward the open door. I see no point in resisting at this point. I have useless arms. I'm worthless, without value. Maybe they're going to use me as the main ingredient in some sort of alien glue.

Through the doorway, I expect to catch a glimpse of the alien landscape. No. It's a room with no windows and no doors. Maybe this is a Wellesian society, forced to live underground to escape the pollution they have created on the surface of their planet. But then they would have no eyes. And there would be no need for all these fluorescent lights. Why won't they let me see the new planet? I'll bet in all their rush to welcome me, they just plain forgot to include it in their itinerary. The alien mayor will present me with the key to the city, we'll all go out to some fine alien revolving restaurant at a downtown hotel. Right.

In this next room, there is a small man behind the desk, at an enormous IBM Selectric typewriter. IBM doesn't stand for International Business Machines, it's INTERGALACTIC Business Machines, I get it. They've been trading with the aliens for years now, I'm sure. I check the telephone, and it says Pacific Bell. Of course, the bell of peace, bridging the gap between our culture and theirs. It's definitely fitting into the puzzle. He accepts a piece of paper from the pinchy boot stomper and begins typing onto some sort of carbon paper. The end result is a rather unattractive piece of jewelry, which he presents to me.

"Here, put this on, and don't lose it, or you'll be in really big trouble."

I have learned better than to disobey these folks. I look at the bracelet, which reads "Ethan Lloyd, Inmate No. 773,855." Inmate? That is not a pleasant term for a visitor. I'm starting to feel that old fear seep in. I have to relax. They came all the way to the Hotel to find me, so they must want me for some purpose. I look at my hands, and see that one of them is still clutching tightly onto the portrait of the president. Of course, they want me to be president when I'm ready. How could I mistake all this gruff treatment for anything other than a test of my endurance and tolerance? I quickly remember my manners. As I put on the bracelet, I say "Thank you, sir."

"You're welcome." He smiles at me through his glasses, which reflect the fluorescent lights. I squint as I look at them and they send me another message. Once again, the message is planted deep in my brain, and I'll probably get it later.

He holds up my instamatic camera. "Is this yours?" I am somewhat bewildered, unsure how he got it. Maybe the first aliens picked it up in the hotel. I nod yes, and he puts it into a manila envelope. "Sign here." He hands me a blue pen and I sign along a thick black line just below where the flap meets the paper. I hope I didn't do anything stupid just then. Lord knows what they'll figure out to do with my signature.

I turn to leave, and the cock pincher grabs me very tightly by the arm. I pull out my old prep school charm again, "Excuse me sir, but you're hurting me."

The magic words. He relaxes his grip enough to let blood circulate. I can control them through manners. "Please escort me to the hotel, I'm afraid this is my first time here."

This causes both the pincher and the typer to start laughing. Things are starting to look up. I laugh along with them, in a reserved sort of Lockjaw laugh that seems even funnier once I am doing it. I would not look out of place at a luncheon with all the republicans that gasped in horror at me in the lobby of the Mark Hopkins.

"Mmmmhmmmhmmm, yes, to the hotel, thank you."

Pincher boy opens another doorway, and points to a room with three brick walls. The front is a cage. "Here's your room, sir."

"Thank you" I try to hide the look of dismay from him. The last thing I need now is a breach in etiquette. "You are too, too kind, dear boy."

He chuckles to himself and shakes his head as he unlocks the cage door, and gently but firmly pushes me in. Then he locks the door. I am inside the room, and he is outside of it. This doesn't feel right. "I must have forgotten to ask the front desk man for my key. Would you be so kind as to go fetch it for me, dear?"

"I'll be right back." He barely contains an unspoken snarl as he tips his hat at me. I guess my manners aren't up to snuff. I think I can charm my way out of this situation, though. He saunters off toward the front desk, but he takes another door, that leads into a room full of aliens dressed in dark blue uniforms. As the door swings shut, I can hear him telling my story between guffaws. I guess he likes me. Pretty soon, I can hear through the door as all the aliens are laughing. My charm worked.

*

The room leaves a lot to be desired. There is a wire bed, with a thin foam mattress and no pillow. In the corner is a sink and a toilet with no seat and no paper, with shit streaming down the sides. The walls are covered in graffiti. I check my messages. None. I can't make out anything. I feel really tired. I lay down on the wire bed and try to make myself comfortable. It's not comfortable. I lay awake, with my eyes staring at the ceiling. There are voices coming from the next room, but I am all alone in here. Why am I all alone?

Several hours pass, I am unable to sleep, and my sense of isolation is building. I don't know where the information comes from, but I know what I'm doing here. They are going to leave me here until I die. They are. I just realized it. No mayor, no key to the city, no presidency, I'm going to stay here in this yellow filth-encrusted quadrangle of squalor until I die and even after the putrefaction has eaten away the flesh from my bones, my skeleton will stay in this cage. This requires immediate action.

"LET ME OUT!!!" I scream so hard it hurts my ears. There is no response. "HELP!!! LET ME OUT!!!" The echo off the walls makes my ears ring and my throat starts to burn. It might be because of the bad air on this planet. "PLEASE HELP ME!!!!" No one can hear me. I bang my fists as hard as I can into the cage, but they only make a dull thud, and the metal vibrates. This might not be a good idea. Dark purple bruises appear on my hands. "FUCK YOU ALL!!! LET ME THE FUCK OUT OF HERE!!!"

A uniformed alien pokes his head through the door that leads to the room full of laughing aliens. "Shut up."

He slams the door behind him. The sense of doom I'm feeling is so profound that I sink right into it. The light in my cell changes color. I can't see color anymore. The yellow cell turns black and white. My fists are giant purple welts. No one cares. Why isn't my mother here to take care of me? Why am I all alone in this godforsaken pit on some unknown planet? What did I do to deserve this? The last time I felt anywhere near this lonely was driving the road between El Paso and San Antonio in the middle of the night. I would give anything to be there now. I want to go home. "I WANT TO GO HOME!!!" Nothing, just my own voice ringing in my ears.

I will never see Texas again. The new planet is not such a friendly place. I take out the dollar bill that the pincher cop gave me and I examine it for any clues. It doesn't look like I remember dollar bills to look. The ink moves around if I stare directly at it. There are little red and blue fibers, which, upon close inspection, wriggle like worms. The picture of George Washington is the same, as far as I can tell. I fold the top half of his head down over the ruffle of his neckline and make a mushroom, just like I used to do in elementary school. I don't know why, but this provides me with some comfort. There is nothing to do in this yellow prison cell. The toilet has no seat, so you can bet I'm not going to take a shit in here. They probably have security cameras watching me.

Just at the moment I look over at the toilet and think about flushing myself down, I suppress a giggle. But then there is a loud guffaw from the next room. They are reading my thoughts and impressions as I am left in isolation, like some rat in a medical experiment. I wish there was some way I could block them from reading my private thoughts, but I think the only way to do that is to scream.

"LET ME THE FUCK OUT OF HERE!"

If I keep screaming, they won't be able to read my thoughts, but I will go hoarse as well. I may need my voice to reason with the ones who aren't reading my thoughts directly. There is nobody helpful here, just a bunch of uniformed fascist pigs.

CHAPTER 7

I don't know how long I've been here. I have no means of keeping track of time, which is different on a different planet anyway. I think it was three quarters of an hour ago that somebody shoved a plate full of greasy chicken and soggy green beans through the grate. I didn't touch it, in case it was poisoned, or worse, bugged. They want me to eat it so they can further read my thoughts. There is a transmitter embedded in each bean. I don't want to inspect them, because they will be all over me with more boots and insults. This planet blows.

Finally, a uniform comes to the cell door.

"Turn around, I gotta cuff you." Even though I don't trust this guy further than I can spit, I go ahead and turn around. He cuffs me through the grate. He opens the gate and motions me out.

"C'mon, we're going upstairs." Whatever that means. It sounds pretty important. I guess I'm going to get the treatment deserving of a visitor to this planet after all. We go back out the doorway past the man with the glasses and the typewriter. He flashes me again with those glasses. What the fuck is he telling me? It's like I can feel the message entering my brain, but I can't interpret it yet. Maybe it will come to me in my dreams. It occurs to me that the feeling I am having might not be thoughts being planted, but thoughts being removed. They're amnesia glasses.

I'm so tired of being mistreated, I don't care what they do with my thoughts. My throat is swollen from all the shouting I did. I am happy to resign myself to whatever cruel torture they have in store for me next.

Out another door, and we're in a wide hallway and up a long flight of stairs. I can catch glimpses out of the wired glass windows in each door. At the first level, I can see what looks like an airport, with lots of x-ray machines. Beyond that I can see the light of the new planet, harsh and unforgiving. It looks like I would burn up in the white heat of the alien sun. I'd better not try to make a break for it.

At the next landing I can see out the door into a narrow hallway filled with glass-encased message boards, like the kind you see on the front of a church. It almost looks like a hallway at Columbia University. Maybe it's just a mirror into my past, not a window at all.

The flights of stairs continue, for what seems like an eternity. I haven't climbed this many steps since the Statue of Liberty. I was eleven years old. Finally, we reach the top level. We walk into the middle of a large room, filled with earthlings. I am so exhausted, I can no longer stand, and I collapse in a heap in the middle of the floor.

I lay my head to the concrete and stare at it. It is moving slowly, like lizard skin. The cracks stretch out like slow moving snakes, then disappear. The room is steaming hot and filled with talking. All of the earthlings are talking among themselves. One approaches me. He is black, very black. He is speaking so fast I can't understand what he's saying. It's hurting my ears to listen to him. He kicks me. I turn to look at him. His voice is coming out faster than his mouth is moving. He laughs to himself, then launches into another tirade. I can pick up random insults in his speech. He calls me "motherfucker, cracker, bitch." I don't know for sure what to do. I am so weak; I can barely lift my head. I haven't had any water or food in quite a while. I decide it's best to ignore him. The whole room is watching our exchange. He does not stop. My temptation to turn and insult him back is clearly misguided, and I do not follow it.

Periodically, a large matron opens the door and calls names. I consult the tag around my wrist, which still says "Ethan Lloyd." After she calls the names, the person disappears behind the glass wall. They don't return. The man has not stopped talking the entire time. This area is highly unsupervised. There is a fat alien cop standing guard, but he fails to take an interest in the skirmish which is developing between me and this insane man. I feel something in my pocket. It's the dollar bill. At that exact moment, they call another name. I make the connection. They are interviewing us for the presidency. George Washington, of course! It makes sense now. But I am not going to make it to the presidency interview if this man keeps insulting me. I can't even move from my supine position. I reach into my pocket and take out the dollar bill. This causes the man to quiet down for a moment, before he launches back into his incomprehensible insulting tirade. I hold the bill near him, and it quiets him again for a second. This is a magic dollar bill, for sure. I finally speak.

I hold the dollar bill out, and very slowly and deliberately say, "Here...take this...and shut the fuck up." He snatches it away from me, and walks away. It worked; the magic dollar bill shut him up. But what was I thinking? That was supposed to be the ticket to the presidency. I've blown my candidacy. At that exact moment, they call "Duane Harris." The talking man looks at me and laughs as he walks through the doorway.

Dread washes over me in one long shudder. I've just blown my chance to be president. I just gave away my golden ticket to political power to Duane Harris. He's in there telling them about it right now. Using all my strength, I lift myself from the floor. The last wave of dread must have given me some adrenaline, because I feel some of my strength returning. I look through the glass at the scene unfolding. Duane is talking to a large alien woman. He turns and sees me, and starts laughing and pointing. It's over. He was a spy sent by the presidency commission to test my stamina. This whole thing has been a test, and I failed. I never failed anything in school until just this past year, when I dropped out of Columbia with D's and F's. Now it seems to be a habit. I am a failure. I hang my head in sorrow. I sit next to another black man, and start to cry. He takes an interest in me.

"Are you okay, man?"

I lift my head to answer him, and when I look into his eyes, I see that he is wall-eyed. He's not an earthling, he's an alien. But there is unconditional love in his eyes. He takes my hand and says "You're gonna be okay."

"Ethan Lloyd," it's my name from the mouth of the matron.

He gives my hand another reassuring squeeze, and then I get up and walk into the room. That was the first moment of kindness I have experienced since I got to this planet. I hope there are other aliens like him. The good ones, they're the ones with one eye looking at me and one eye cast toward the heavens.

I step through the glass partition, and the air temperature changes quite drastically. It's cool in this room. The large woman to whom Duane had been talking is now sitting before me. She takes my right thumb and rolls it across an ink pad, and roughly rolls it from one side to the other on a piece of card paper with little partitions on it. She repeats the procedure with my index finger, and all the fingers of my right hand. Then she does it with my left hand. I am nervous about the test for president. How am I going to pass it if I gave away the ticket? I feel like I showed up for the SAT but forgot my driver's license.

"Excuse me, ma'am, but I appear to have lost my ticket for the test."

"Huh?" She wrinkles her nose at me.

"Never mind." I really shouldn't offer them any more information unless they ask me directly.

"Lemme see your wristband."

I hold it out to her. She types my name on a sheet of paper. There appear to be a lot of names on this list. They know who I am. She cross-references my name in a folder. "Oh boy, you're in big trouble – trespassing." She giggles. I am not aware of being a trespasser on this planet. If I am not mistaken, I am a victim of a cosmic kidnapping. No sense in arguing with her.

"Hey Jim, we've got a trespasser!" Jim looks like an orangutan. He has red fur on his forearms, and his face is long and ugly. "Put him with the misdemeanors," she instructs him.

Jim says nothing. He waltzes me into a corridor, where he instructs me to remove my clothing with crude hand signals. I take my shirt off. Jim lifts my arms and inspects my armpits.

"Now the pants." I am shocked. He speaks. I remove my pants. He pulls my underwear down and spreads my ass cheeks. I turn and look at him. He has a flashlight between his teeth. This is not part of the presidential examination.

"Are you from the phone company?" I ask him. He frowns at me and hands me an orange pantsuit. He has gathered my clothes, the last vestige of my life on earth, and he places them in a pouch with my name on it. At least I got to keep my underwear. I put the suit on. He throws me little foam slippers to wear as shoes. I put them on, although they are uncomfortable.

He grabs me somewhat gruffly by the arm and escorts me down a narrow hallway, which has wired glass windows that look in on the room with the inkpads. At the end of the greasy hallway there is an iron door with bars on it, behind which there sits a ragtag assortment of earthlings. One of them has a mohawk. Oh good, at least I will have a friend to talk to. He pushes me through the doorway. A large man with a red beard comes up to the gate.

"Hey man, when do I get my phone call?" He obviously is here for the same reasons I am, a direct result of the conspiracy of the great ATT corporation.

Flashlight Jim looks at him and snarls, "Sit the fuck back down."

The man with the beard points at him and jabs his finger in the air for emphasis as he shouts, "Nobody fucking tells me what to do. Fuck you man!" He takes a swing at the air, which ends up landing on the side of my head. I fall down. It feels good there, so I just stay there. Aliens suck; earthlings are worse.

My vision is a little out of focus for a minute or two. As I regain my clarity of vision, I realize I am staring at a bare mattress. Just in front of the mattress is a bare foot. The toenails are encrusted with mud and slime. I raise my eyes a little to see the owner of the toenails. It's the mohawk boy. I look up at him and smile.

"Did you fuck with the phone company too?"

He doesn't answer. His eyes twitch. He has just signaled me not to talk about it, because the place is bugged. I raise my eyebrows toward him and mouth a silent "Sorry." He seems not to notice. I wish there was better company here. I feel like I've fallen in with some really bad earthlings. That must be for cussing out so many people. Fine. I look at my identification badge and it worries me. I have really small hands, and I can wriggle out of a lot of things. I carefully tug on the band until I can squeeze it over my thumb base. It cuts lightly into my skin, drawing a small amount of blood. Nobody is watching. Nobody cares. I tug a little further and it is wedged fairly firmly on the lump of my thumb. The mohawk guy sneers at me, "Don't do that man, you'll never get out of here."

"Fuck off." I don't know why I said it, I just did.

BAM! I feel the dirty toenails make contact with the side of my head.

"Fucking Faggot, leave your wrist band on."

This interchange attracts the attention of Flashlight Jim, who opens the gate to the cell to see what's going on. The bearded man leaps into action, punching Flashlight Jim in the face. It has very little effect. During this interchange, I manage to slip the wristband off completely, with only a little bit of blood. There, I've managed to shed my identity. There is a huge fracas going on just inches away from my face. Beard Man is down on the floor, Flashlight Jim is holding his head there with his foot. Blood oozes out of Redbeard's mouth. It looks like he got kicked pretty bad. While the commotion is in full swing, I get up slowly, and approach the bare mattress. There is a hole in the side, and I shove my identification band into the hole. It is gobbled up by the spun polyester insides. They will never know who I am again. I was pretty sure they didn't want me to be president anyway. Who fucking cares? I am free now. I approach the jail cell door and prepare to walk out. It doesn't budge. I concentrate really hard, and the electronic lock comes undone. I open the door, but two alien guards come running down the hallway. One grabs me as I head out the door.

"Who left this unlocked!?" screams the guard who grabbed me. He pushes me back inside the cell. Escape is never easy. There is the sound of metal clicking. The bearded prisoner is handcuffed and unconscious. One of the guards help Jim to drag him away to some distant solitary cell, where he will undoubtedly reside for the rest of his miserable existence on this terrible new planet.

The fracas is over, but the guard who grabbed me as I was escaping points right at me. "You, you're going to solitary." What in the hell did I do?

"I was just on my way home, actually," I assert. The guard guffaws at this one as he clamps my wrists with handcuffs. He doesn't notice that I have no wristband. He leads me out the gate that I had tried to exit before, and down the hallway lined with cells. This is my new home. Fabulous. He puts me in a room with nothing but a sink and a toilet and a bare mattress and shuts the door. I look around me at the plain white walls. I think I'm dead. I'm dead. I am in purgatory. I will wait here for the rest of my conscious existence, which may very well be forever. Suddenly, this strikes me as a very sad situation. My eyes sting just before the tears run down my face. I have never felt this alone in my whole life. I can't control my sobbing. My conscious self is locked in a cell in what I had mistaken for a new planet. I'm in a waiting room for oblivion. I look down, half expecting my body to be missing. It's there, but I can't feel it. I lie back on my bed and prepare for eternity. I am dead. My heart isn't beating. I'd better call my Grandmother and let her know. There is a telephone in my cell, put there by the phone company. I pick up the receiver and it makes that horrible sound a phone makes that has been left off the hook for more than sixty seconds. It hurts my ear. I can't get an outside line. I can't reach my Grandmother. Now the tears come worse than before, and my nose starts to drip down the front of my face. I lie on the bed and drown in snot and tears.

*

Hours pass, each one feeling like an entire day. Someone shoves a plate of food under the door to my cell. I take it but I won't eat it. They might have poisoned it or planted devices to monitor my brainwaves in the mashed potatoes. I take the red sauce from the noodles and try to write something to Wanda on the wall. The words won't stay, they keep falling off. I can't reach her anymore. I am definitely dead. No point in eating.

*

The lights just went out. I can't see anything. I have no tears left to cry in my head.

*

I don't remember sleeping, but the last time I checked it was still dark in this room, and now it's light and there's someone in the cell standing over me. I focus my eyes and Flashlight Jim comes into focus.

"Get up, we're moving you to the main floor." I get to leave purgatory, hurrah. I instinctively reach to get my things and realize that I don't have any things. This makes me sad again and I start to cry. Flashlight Jim puts his hand on my shoulder and says, "Don't let them see you cry, man. They'll eat you alive."

Out the door, down a flight of steps, we arrive in a large cell with lots of smaller cells inside it. There is a hoot and a whistle from one of the cells. I look inside, and it's the man with the beard from yesterday. He shouts, "Hey buddy, we're gonna be cell mates."

Great. I get to stay with the winner of the idiot pageant. Flashlight Jim opens the cell door with a magnetic key and puts me inside. The door closes. I feel a hand on my ass. I turn around and face the bearded man.

"Sweet. Real sweet." He admires my ass. "You ever been in jail before, sweetheart?" His breath smells like camphor. I shake my head no. I don't want him to hear me speak. I also don't feel like informing him that this is not jail, but hell.

"You don't speak?"

I shake my head no, and make some fake sign language at him. He chuckles. "We're gonna have a good time, you and me. Now let me teach you the first lesson in prison. Always make your buddy's bunk for him." He points to the bed, the top bunk of course, and waits expectantly for me to make his bed. I don't know how to make a bed without fitted sheets. I take all the covers off the bed and stuff them under the mattress. I feel something hit me on the side of the head. It's Redbeard's hand.

"Not like that, are you a moron?"

I nod yes. My retarded deaf person act has an effect on him. He takes pity on me. "Never mind, man. I'll do it myself." He shoves me out of the way and proceeds to make the bed in military fashion. It looks like you could bounce a quarter on it. My bed is bare, the two paper sheets and wool blanket are folded on top of the bunk. I throw the sheets on the ground and wrap myself in the scratchy wool blanket. I curl up on the bare mattress and close my eyes.

CHAPTER 8

I can't sleep. I close my eyes, and when I open them, many hours have passed, but I haven't slept. Sometimes I can leap forward in time without even closing my eyes. Redbeard is snoring right now. I don't know what time it is, but all the lights are off. I walk over to the door to my cell. I put my hand up to the magnetic lock and concentrate. It clicks. I open the door and wander out into the open area. There are concrete picnic tables where the men eat their suppers. I stretch out on the top of one of the tables and close my eyes.

My eyes open, it is daylight and there is a whooping sound. Everyone is banging on their cell doors and shouting at me.

"Hey man, how did you get out there!?"

"Let me out too."

I turn my head just in time to receive a blow from Flashlight Jim. The crash of his fist reverberates in my ears like a cymbal. I see two of everything. I am conscious but I can't stand up. He drags me back to my cell, unlocks the gate and drags me in, leaving me stretched out on the floor (like a patient etherised on a table, Prufrock, Eliot. Earth.)

The ringing sound that started with Flashlight Jim's hammer to my head does not go away. It makes me nauseous. I throw up into the seatless toilet in the corner of the cell. As the vomit flows out of me and into the bowl, I silently pray that my soul will go with it, and when I flush it away, I will be with it, flowing down the endless river toward a new and happy self.

Flashlight Jim comes back. I cower in the corner.

"Show me your ID, I need to make a report." Ha!! Fat Fucker, he'll never find out who I am. I hold up my empty wrists and smile. A thorough search of my cell reveals nothing. He is quite flustered.

"We're gonna have to find out who you are, mister, or you ain't gettin' out of here." I don't answer him; I don't need to. I will just wait until the middle of the night, and I'll unlock my door and go home. Wherever that is.

A few hours have gone by, and there's quite a bit of buzz in and around my cell. Silence is a very powerful tool in fighting these fascist alien bastards. A man in a suit shoves a clipboard under my nose and asks me to indicate my identity off of a list of names. The list is pretty impressive. One name on the list is Jesus Martinez, which strikes me as a pretty nice name and I choose it. This doesn't go over too well.

"Damn, he's playing with us." They leave me in my cell, with Redbeard, who has buddied up to me since my first escape. He is hoping I am going to help him get out of here. Well, he'll have to make my bed for a thousand nights before I am letting him ride out of here with me. It's lunchtime, and there's a flavorless colorless broth with chunks of imitation earth vegetables floating around in a sea of noodles made out of library paste and cigarette filters. The other inmates seem pretty happy to eat it, but I refuse. I nibble on the edge of a biscuit. Somebody asks if they can have my soup, and they take my silence as an implied affirmative. The soup has mind control drugs in it.

I return to my bed and close my eyes. When I open them, the cell is closed and the lights are off. Redbeard is snoring very loudly. I approach the cell door and close my eyes. I concentrate. The lock clicks and I enter the main area. I go to the cell door that contains this common area. It doesn't unlock. There's a telephone beside it, and I dial a combination of numbers into it. It spits out a nasty sound. I hold the receiver as close to the door as I can and broadcast the beeping sound. The lock clicks, I am free.

The hallway has one fluorescent light for every 20 yards or so. I creep through the shadows, invisible. I slink into a doorway as a black guard rounds the corner. He walks right past me. I am invisible in this doorway. I have to sneeze, and I close my mouth and cover my nose to suppress it. Although there was only a slight change in my breathing, the sound catches the attention of the guard who is perhaps thirty yards away. He whirls around and shines his flashlight right at me. I run as fast as I can down the hallway. I am wearing the slippers they gave me when I put on the orange suit, and they don't have much traction. As I round the corner, I see a black woman in a nurse's uniform behind a thick panel of bulletproof glass, just before I lose my grip on the floor and slide onto my side. The woman must help me. I stand up and pound on the glass, and she looks up. One of her eyes is askew, looking skyward. She is one of the good, helpful aliens. With her telepathic mind, she tells me her name is Grace. She makes me feel safe and warm with her thoughts that she plants in my mind.

"Help me please!" I scream. Suddenly I feel a hand grabbing my wrist behind me and wrenching my arm halfway out of its socket. The black face of the guard leans into mine, and his breath smells of green onions and garlic salt.

"Just where in the hell do you think you're going." He has one wall-eye too. He's a friend.

I smile at him and say "I'm going home."

"Let's see about that." The nurse comes out from behind her glass window with a hypodermic needle, which she injects into my arm. The lights go out.

*

I haven't slept, but a lot of time seems to have passed. It's daylight, and my eyes are coming into focus. I hear the familiar clacking of an electric typewriter. The nurse is in the next room. A wall of metal bars separates me from her. I am so glad she is taking care of me, tears of relief pour down my face. I try to stand up, but can't. I lie back down. My head is ringing, either from Flashlight Jim's fist or Nurse Grace's needle. The nurse spins around in her swivel chair and peers in at me through the bars.

"You up?"

"Yep."

"What's your name, honey?"

I don't answer. I know she's a helper alien, but I don't want any of the other aliens to hear me. I try to send my name to her with my mind, but her receiver is off. She lets out a long sigh and returns to her typing. I lie back and stare at the ceiling. She types and talks with her back to me in a soft voice, "Now hon, we ain't gonna be able to let you go if you don't tell us your name."

*

Another time warp, it's much later on, according to the clock above Nurse Grace's head. The man with the suit is talking with her. He has the same clipboard. He turns and sees my open eyes. Both his eyes are looking right at me. He's not a friend. He pokes his head into the cell and asks me, politely, "Are you ready to tell us your name now?"

I politely refuse by shaking my head in the negative. He withdraws and turns to the nurse.

"Fifty-one fifty him."

What does that mean? She turns around toward me and she has a great big smile on her face. She tells me with her thoughts that it's going to be okay, so I relax. Fifty-one fifty. I'll be okay.

What else could they do to me at this point? My arm is still throbbing from being wrenched halfway out of the socket. I might already be dead, in which case they can't kill me. I think they're planning what body I will be born into in the next life. Death is such a tedious bureaucracy. She has all these papers for me to sign, which I do, with an X. I don't want them to know who I am.

A pink-faced man in a police uniform appears at the door.

He opens the door to my cell and puts handcuffs on me. He walks me out of the room and to an elevator. We ride in the elevator. I look at him. He gives off a friendly vibe. I hope he will be my father in the next life.

"Are you my new father?" I ask him. Oddly enough, he doesn't say anything at all to me. He doesn't acknowledge my question. The elevator doors open, and we're in a parking garage with police cars. How strange. The doors have six pointed stars on them, like the Star of David. He puts me in the back of one of the Jewish police cars.

"Am I going home?" I hope he'll answer me. He turns to me and says, "Not exactly."

I'm worried. They have ways of springing big surprises on me here, and I'm not willing to tolerate another one. He sees the panic in my face and says, "It'll be a lot better than this hell-hole, that's for sure." Then he turns back and starts the ignition on the car. He puts it in reverse and backs out of the parking space. I see light; it's the exit to the garage. He drives toward it. I am being reborn. The sunlight is too bright. There is no doctor to smack me on my bottom. I look down at my body, fully expecting to be an infant, but I seem to be the same person I was before.

"Where are we going?"

"General."

What in the hell does that mean? This guy gives better answers than almost anyone I've met so far, and they still suck.

I close my eyes, and when I open them again, we're in a giant parking lot. Pink-face stops the car and gets out, walking around to my door. He opens it and asks me to step out. I get up, barely able to stand, shivering in the early morning fog. My orange suit is too thin to protect me from the elements. I haven't breathed real air in a few days, at least. I fill my lungs and exhale, smiling. Pink-face leads me by the cuffs toward a sliding glass door on the side of a giant concrete building. The doors slide open automatically, and we're inside a lobby. There are rows of chairs in the lobby, all of them empty.

There is a desk, manned by a thin white woman in librarian spectacles. She smiles at me as I approach the counter. I lean up against the counter, breathless, and smile at her.

"Hello, who do we have here?"

"Won't give a name," says Pink-face.

"Well, this is going to be very difficult. Do you want to give me your name, young man?" As much as I do, I am afraid that they will have some nasty surprise waiting for me as soon as they have me identified. All the walls will melt away and I'll be back in the prison, duped by a hologram. There is a phone on the desk, and it rings. The lady with the glasses picks it up.

"Yes? I see. Right away, doctor." She puts the phone down. "I have to see Dr. Vile for a moment, if you could just have a seat." As she turns her back to me, I make a grab for the phone. I haven't heard a dial tone in days. The phone has a dial tone. Pink-face slaps the receiver out of my hand. The noise causes the librarian woman to turn around.

"No, let him use the phone."

Is this a trick? I don't care anymore. I need to talk to

Grandma. I need to tell her that I didn't mean to solve the puzzle. I really should have left it all alone. Pink-face hands me the phone. I dial 1, the area code, the number. It's ringing!

"Hello?" It's Grandma! She answered.

"Grandma, it's me."

"Where have you been?"

"I don't know."

The receiver is snatched from me by a man in a doctor's coat. Where did he come from? Tears well up in my eyes. I can't help myself.

"Please! Let me have it back!" I lash out toward the doctor, trying to get the phone back. Out of nowhere, two large men appear. They wrestle me to the floor. I can see out of the corner of my eye that the doctor is talking to my Grandmother. I want my Grandma.

"Grandma! Help me!!" The librarian comes at me with a hypodermic needle. I try to get away, but the two men are infinitely stronger than I am. Where's a chunk of kryptonite when you need it? I feel a sharp pain in my buttocks, and instantly everything gets very fuzzy. It doesn't go black, it just slows down. The men peel me up off of the floor. I can't really hold my head up anymore. I am as a limp as a freshly run-over snake.

*

I can't tell what they're doing, because I can't lift my head off of the table. I'm on my back on a table, and there is a leather smell.

I feel leather going around my wrists. I am on a table, I already said that, but I have to keep telling myself that, or I might slide into something. The fluorescent lights hurt my eyes. Did somebody hear my thoughts? The lights just went off and the door closed. There's a tiny window in the door, and that is all that is letting light into my space. I feel like I should be scared, but my brain hurts too much to care. I drift down a very uncomfortable river toward what might be sleep.

CHAPTER 9

I am pretty sure I slept this time. Someone came in and undid my cuffs. I'm still on the table, but the room has changed. There are curtains suspended from metal tracks, which hang from the ceiling, surrounding my bed. I hear people talking in the distance. I think someone gave me a lobotomy. I feel for the scar, but nothing is there. My brain won't make any connections. It's taking everything I've got just to lay here and think this shit. I close my eyes, and the world goes black for a while.

When I open my eyes again, someone is shaking me. It's my dad. What is he doing here? I can't see him clearly because I don't have enough energy to focus my eyes. "Hey there, how are you feeling?" he asks me awkwardly. Summoning all the energy I can humanly muster, I open my mouth and say, "yucky." Then I close my eyes. When I open them again, he's gone. Was he just a hallucination? I can't really tell.

The curtains are drawn back by a dusky brown arm with a small brown fist with white palms. I can't turn my head to see who owns the arms, but then she fills the frame of my vision. She has metal-rimmed glasses and a kind smile.

"How are we feeling?" Her voice is soft.

"Bad."

"Bad?"

"Bad. Who are you?"

"I'm Barbara. Do you want to come to the day room?"

The thought of lifting my legs is discouraging. "No."

"No? Okay, then. You missed breakfast. Do you want a snack to keep you until lunch?"

I turn my attention inward for a moment, and discover that my stomach is growling. "Yeah."

She leaves the frame of my vision and I hear her footsteps pattering down a hard linoleum hallway toward the source of food. Where the fuck am I? In a few moments, she returns with a plastic orange juice with a tight foil top, and a packet of cheez n' crackers. She reaches behind me. A motor purrs and I feel myself swinging into a sitting position. My eyes won't move in their sockets, they're all dried out. I close my lids, and it feels like sandpaper. They start to water, and this loosens the rust and I can rotate them. I appear to be in a room made out of curtain fabric. I am in a bed with metal railings and cheap acrylic blankets. The sheets are mostly polyester, and they slide across the plastic surface of the mattress as my weight shifts. I am wearing a white gown flocked with little blue starbursts. She opens the top of the orange juice and I hold the rough plastic edge to my lips. It cuts the corners of my mouth and they sting as the acidic juice spills out the sides. It tastes like diesel exhaust. I guess I'm still in space. The juice doesn't taste like juice back home. I can't make a tight enough grip to get the top off the Cheez n' Crackers, so she does it for me.

"There you go."

"Who are you?"

"I'm Barbara Hall, your day nurse." I think she told me that before. "You seem to be managing okay. I'll be just down the hall if you need me."

Hall down the hall. It's some kind of code, and if I figure it out, this aching feeling in my legs and arms will go away, and my brain will stop hurting. I'll work on it in a minute. The Cheez n' Crackers don't taste very nice. The salt from the crackers burns the edges of my mouth where the orange juice cup cut into them. I can't stand not knowing where I am.

Mustering as much strength as I have, I swing my legs off the bed and rotate until I am sitting up of my own accord. It feels like gravity is much stronger in this place. There are lots of voices beyond the curtain, in the "hall" as she called it. My feet have little foam slippers on them, just like in the place where I was dressed in orange. But now I'm dressed in blue. I wonder where they'll let me wear green. I don't want to wear red. On the edge of the curtain there is a caduceus. Two snakes climb a pole. One of the snakes was in me earlier. I reach out my hand and touch the snake, and it gives me energy. I take hold of the curtain and use it as a hand grip to get me to my feet. My knees are wobbly, but I manage to stand with the snake energy as an aid. I peek my head through the curtain, and there's just a dimly lit room with a door that opens onto a hallway. I patter slowly toward the door, which is propped open with one of those rubber doorjambs.

Outside the door, there are many people dressed like me, in blue-flocked gowns. There are also people in regular clothing, corduroy, sweaters, sneakers. Barbara Hall is in the bunch. She's wearing a yellow sweater and wool gabardine slacks. Her clothing distinguishes her from the blue-clad masses. I can't see very well; my eyes are having trouble focusing. My head is throbbing, but it's not a headache, it feels very different. It's a thoughtache. No one sees me; maybe I'm invisible.

*

There is a blinding flash, and now it's nighttime. I'm on the bed, the curtains are open. To my right there is a table on rollers. On the table there is a rectangular chunk of plastic divided into two halves, one on top of the other. They look like they can be separated. I reach out with my right hand and feel the table. It's real. Why did I doubt myself? I pull the table to the bed, and inspect the plastic. There is a piece of paper attached to the plastic. It's a green piece of paper with a drawing of a cornucopia on it. There are typed rows with names of different kinds of food. Somebody put circles around the food with a red pen. At the bottom of the paper there is an aphorism: "an apple a day keeps the doctor away!" It seems harmless enough until I turn the paper over and there is my name, last name first. How did it get there? What are they trying to do to me?

Underneath the top piece of plastic there is cold food. It looks much better than the things they gave me in the containment facility. There is turkey with mashed potatoes and gravy. I touch the gravy. It is solid, like jam. They are trying to fool me into thinking this is earth food. I inspect the food for any listening devices. There are tiny flecks that look like pepper on the potatoes. They are little microphones. I'm hungry. I scrape all the microphones off the potatoes, along with the solid lump of gravy-like goo. The potatoes taste like the kind that comes from a box. There are more microphones on the turkey. The gravy peels off like freshly dried paint from a mirror. The turkey is sliced very thin, with no skin. It could just as well be made from soybeans. The texture is not like real turkey. It resembles the lunchmeat turkey that comes in plastic pouches at the grocery store. I have no tangible proof that this is turkey. I am so hungry I really don't care at this point. If they are trying to torture me some more, putting poison in the turkey, I am willing to find out. So far, so good. Maybe it's slow acting poison.

*

There is another bright flash, and I'm lying in the bed, but there are leather straps around my arms. Barbara the nurse is in my face. She appears to be reprimanding me.

"You can get out of these just as soon as you calm down, mister."

What is she talking about? She is making me feel very angry. How did I get here? I want to go and eat my turkey. The straps are preventing me from leaving. I glare at Barbara. Why is she doing this to me? There is a glob of oatmeal on the curtain near me. A bowl lies upside down on the floor. A river of milk and melted butter runs from the bowl toward Barbara's feet. If she doesn't move, it's going to get on her patent leather shoes. I don't think I'll tell her. It's daylight outside.

*

These flashes are getting irritating. Now I'm sitting down in a large room filled with other people in gowns. We're watching television. I'm standing at a counter. On the counter there is a pile of tobacco and cigarette papers. Somebody nudges me from behind.

"Hey, Ethan, are you going to eat your lunch? Are you?"

I turn to see who nudged me. It's a tall boy with very closely cropped hair. His eyes are heavy lidded. I realize that I can't really turn my head as easily as I just tried to do. My neck is very stiff. I have to slowly twist my body back into position.

"Cause I want your apple if you're not going to eat it."

He can have my apple. He can have whatever he wants. He has a hand-poked tattoo of a smiley face on his forearm. He knows my name. Who is he?

"Who are you?"

"Jimmy Simple. Damn, Ethan, you can't remember anything, can you? It's the meds. What they got you on anyway?"

"Uh...on? I dunno." I don't particularly remember being here. I have amnesia. As hard as I search my memory banks, I still can't remember what happened just before this. There's a double paned window at the end of the countertop. I can see the skyline of San Francisco out the window. It looks like a shadow box.

Something they manufactured to make me feel more at home.

Jimmy Simple is really cute. He can't stand still. He keeps hopping up and down on one foot and then another. Sometimes he makes little wooshing noises.

"What are you doing?"

He looks at me with a 'duh' stare: "I'm skating. They won't let me have my skateboard in here, so I'm just practicing. Ollies, grinds and tic-tacs, you know."

"Ethan, you have a visitor." A male nurse appears out of nowhere. How does he know who I am? I turn around, and there is my mother. What in the fuck is she doing here?

"Ethan!" She rushes forward and smothers me. The nurse clears his throat.

"I'm sorry ma'am, please obey the rules."

She pulls backs enough so I can see him pointing to a sign that reads 'No Touching.' How molecular. I feel like an electron. My mother turns to the nurse and lets out a vicious snarl.

"What do you mean I can't touch my own son"?

"Rules are rules." She refuses to let me go. She is clutching me so tightly that I am having difficulty breathing.

"Mom, let me go. I can't breathe."

A tall black man approaches us. His nametag says 'Lester' in white letters on a black plastic background.

"What seems to be the problem here? Are we having trouble obeying the rules?"

"We," snaps my mother, "are hugging our son."

"I'm going to have to ask you to refrain from touching him,

ma'am. You're disturbing the other patients." There is a small crowd gathering.

"Let me go, mom." She shoves me away from her. There is a look of wild desperation in her eyes. She looks like she has been crying for ten years. She has gray hairs on her temples. How many years have gone by? Now I know the view out the window is fake, because Mom is in Vermont. How can I see San Francisco out of the window if she's in Vermont. She's an android.

"You're not real. My mother is in Vermont."

"Honey, I flew out here. Your Grandmother called me and told me what happened."

"About the abduction?"

"You were arrested."

I can't take any more of this. Barbara comes by and sticks her smiling face into our discussion.

"Hi, how are we feeling?"

"Don't patronize him." Barbara frowns at my mother's remark. This is fun. They must not have realized what they were getting into when they replicated her from my chromosomes. She's a raving bitch, and now they have to deal with her.

"It's time for your meds." She hands me a small glass of orange juice. This is what's making me feel so shitty. Every time I drink it, I forget what happens.

"No thanks."

Barbara insists: "You have to take them, Ethan."

"No. They make me sick."

"Honey, they're going to make you well." This coming from

Ms. Natural, my mother, strikes me as more than a bit shocking.

"It's poison, mom. I can't"

*

That's the last thing I remember. Now I'm in a different room, with lots of other beds. There are little blue jugs resting on rolling tables. Jimmy Simple is asleep across from me. It seems to be dawn. My face itches, and when I touch it, I realize that I have grown a beard. Ick. I hate beards. I lift my body, with great difficulty, into an upright position. Jimmy Simple is snoring. He looks so cute lying there, with a little puddle of drool on his pillow. I wish I knew why they were keeping me here. I am really of no service to anyone. I can't do my photography here. I can't do much of anything. I get a little memory flash, and it tells me that the bathroom is down the hall. I have morning wood, but no one is around to see it. I tiptoe down the hallway to the bathroom, using the handrail on the wall for support. When I open the door to the bathroom, the mirror greets me. What a shock. All my long beautiful black hair is gone. Someone gave me a haircut. And the beard looks awful. I look homeless. I am homeless. Where am I? What the fuck is going on? I think it's been a long time since I drank any of the sour orange juice that wipes out my memory banks. What was I doing before I got here? I was going to be president. They gave me an ID, which looked like a dollar bill. And the phone company put me in a jail. I guess they want me to be a doctor, so they put me here to study medicine. That makes sense. A doctor. Won't my Grandmother be happy? I'm gonna be a doctor. Because I know where Itt's Att.

I flush the toilet, and watch the yellow piss-water swirl away. My next task is to get rid of this lousy beard. I hate what I see in the mirror. I'm one ugly motherfucker.

Outside the bathroom, there is a dry-erase board, with lots of names running vertically down the side, with numbers across the top. It's a calendar of some kind. The last column is the most interesting; it contains comments. In my comment box, it reads: 'Haldol 25 mg BID. Appt with Vile 6/17.' There is a dry erase marker dangling by a string. I uncap it and write in the remaining space in my comment box: 'I know where Itt's Att.'

I replace the cap and return to my bed.

As I pull the covers over me, I hear a rustling sound. It's Jimmy Simple. I turn my head and look over at him. He's staring at me.

"Hey."

"Hi." I wonder what he wants.

"Ethan, can I have your orange juice at breakfast if you're not going to drink it?"

"Yeah, sure." The word breakfast has no meaning in this place. It's such an earth word. What am I doing here? I want to die, I think.

"Ethan, what are you thinking about?"

"I want to die."

"Don't tell them. They'll keep you here forever." He turns his back to me and starts to snore.

Who the fuck are 'they'? How are 'they' keeping me in this place? What is this place? I'll ask Barbara when she gets here. I close my eyes, and for the first time in a very long time, I feel the sensation of going to sleep.

I open my eyes, and the sun is streaming through the windows. There is a commotion in the next room over. I pitter-patter down the hallway in my gown toward the sound. It's a bunch of people sitting at tables, eating breakfast food from the plastic containers. A man in a dazzling white hat and matching pants with a very black face sees me.

"Name?"

"Ethan"

Here you go, man. He hands me a plastic tray with my name on it, just like the other tray before. But inside there is breakfast. Scrambled eggs, with sausage and potatoes. Sort of. I sit down at a table by myself and poke at the sausage. It seems real enough. There is a plastic spork inside of a plastic bag, with a napkin and salt and pepper, just like back in elementary school. The spork breaks when I try to poke it through the plastic. I manage to get the plastic open. With the broken off remains of the spoon area, I scoop up a bit of egg and put it in my mouth. It tastes like it was made in a replicator. The texture is like a very worn out sponge that has been soaking in dishwater for a week. One of the tines must have fallen into the egg, and it lodges itself between two molars. I reach in and pull it out. My gums are bleeding. Jimmy Simple sees me from across the room, and picks up his tray and heads over to my table. He sits down with me.

"So, can I have your orange juice?"

"Yeah." I hand him the plastic cup with the foil covering. He is genuinely thrilled to have it.

"Ethan, you are so nice. Why are you so nice?"

"Same reason you are."

He thinks about that for a while. The sausage tastes good, if not a bit salty. I feel pretty good right now. It's as if I have my brain back on a temporary loan from the folks who took it.

"Meds. Med time." There's a crier out in the hall, announcing the arrival of the cups of orange juice, the small ones without the foil. People place their plastic trays back on the cart and shuffle toward the cups. That's why I feel so good: I haven't had my little cup of orange juice yet. I wonder if there's some way I can avoid it? My breakfast is not finished. I'll just stay here and finish up. Maybe they won't notice if I don't have any. It is easier to eat the egg sponge stuff with my fingers, so I do. Barbara pokes her head into the breakfast room.

"There you are. It's med time."

"Thank you, I won't be having any."

"I'm afraid you have to, Ethan."

If I argue any more with her, she's going to do something awful with me. I think I'll just follow orders for now, until I can devise a plan to get out of all this. I don't feel particularly strong at the moment. I'm having trouble keeping my thoughts glued to my head. They just sort of fly out and flutter away, pages torn from a notebook. The wind is inside my head, blowing me out to sea. Barbara is approaching me with the tiny cup. She holds it out toward me. What is my plan? I can't have this stuff, it's making me weak. Her hand is within range, so I knock the cup out of her hand.

CHAPTER 10

My head is on the concrete floor, and someone is sticking me with a needle. I feel the jab, and my vision gets blurry. I am dragged along the floor out of the dining room and into a very lonely room. There's a bed in the room. I can't move, so the man who drugged me and dragged me lays me on the table. I can't see much of anything. I feel my hands being tightly cuffed in leather. It will be easier to close my eyes than to keep them open.

I don't know what time it is. If I knew what time it was, I could maybe nail down what's happening and when. My eyes open, and Jimmy Simple is there, smiling.

"Hey." He has a big grin on his face.

"Hey. How did you get here?"

"Easy. I just opened the door."

"How long have I been here?"

"Who cares? It's all the same here anyway." I have to agree with him on that point. Is he just a figment of my imagination? How do I know he's real?

"Touch me. I want to know if you're real."

He grins and rubs my cheek with the back of his hand. He has enormous hands, and the skin on them is rough. I can feel my scraggly beard crackling against his hand. I feel very safe now. He's real.

"Jimmy, can you undo me?" I lift my hands, and the shackles

have fallen away.

"Barbara came here and undid you a long time ago, man. Let's go to breakfast. Can I have your orange juice if you don't want it? Only if you don't want it."

Whatever that shit was they gave me, it sure feels nasty. My legs hurt, and I'm sort of twisted in a knot around my neck. I can't turn my head, and my vision is blurry. Nasty, nasty shit. I can't quite sit up all the way, and Jimmy puts an arm under my legs and one behind my back and lifts me to my feet. He's pretty strong. His face is weird, but there's something really adorable about him. I think I like him, a little. Well, maybe not. He's missing a tooth.

I shuffle in to breakfast, and nobody even looks up from the steaming bowls of gruel. Jimmy sits with me at an empty table, and helps me open the plastic bag surrounding my spork. I don't have enough strength in my hands to even make a fist. Once the spork is out, Jimmy hands it to me. I dip it into my puddle of grey hot cereal.

"Ethan, it's a lot better if you put some milk and margarine in it. And some sugar." Jimmy grabs the milk from the plastic tray, opens it, takes a big gulp of it, and pours some in my cereal. He plops a tiny square glob of margarine in the middle. Then he opens a packet of sugar, a little too vigorously, scattering most of it across the table top. Barbara appears in the doorway, and shakes her finger at him. He acknowledges her with a grunt. What are they communicating to each other? Are they talking about me? Is it a conspiracy? After she leaves, he says, "She's such a bitch."

I consider eating my cereal, even though Jimmy drank some of the milk and got his germs in it. A thought crosses my mind, and I can't stop myself before I say what I'm thinking, "Jimmy, if I eat this cereal, it will be like kissing you."

"What?"

Oh thank god he didn't hear that. "Never mind."

The glob of margarine has become a yellow greasy river and it runs over the edge, right over the top of the milk that just hovers at the brim of the bowl. There is margarine heading straight for me, moving much too fast. It defies gravity. Jimmy reaches over and saves me, putting the napkin, the one that used to live with the spork in the plastic pouch, between me and the yellow threat. I take another quick glance at his hands. He sees me looking at his hands.

"Give me yours." He grabs my hand and holds his palm up against mine. His fingers reach skyward, towering over my little digits. I'm a dwarf. I like the feeling of his hand against mine. His fingers topple over and cover my hand. I am afraid of this closeness. I pretend his fists are boxing gloves, and I move them so that he lightly punches himself on the jaw. Why am I so afraid? He doesn't let go. He just smiles and punches himself with the other hand, my fist a little captive inside of his. Barabara appears again.

"No touching." Jimmy drops my hands, and they fall to my side. He looks at me for a split second longer than I expect him to. He's grinning. I blush and turn to my grey porridge and shovel a spoonful into my mouth. The margarine runs out between the spokes of the spork, and down my chin. When I look up, Jimmy is still looking at me. I turn away really fast. Out of the corner of my eye, I can see his hand reaching for my face. He wipes the margarine off of my face.

"Damn, Ethan, you're really a mess." He punches me in the arm, gently, but it still hurts. He stands up, grabs my orange juice, and walks out of the room.

Time feels more like a comma than a period. , , , , , , Instead of . . . . . It moves forward, hesitates, and moves on. How long has time been doing this? Sometimes I blink, and time moves forward a whole minute or even an hour. Sometimes everyone is frozen and I can move all around them, never knowing when they are going to reactivate. Do I want a PRN of cogentin? Yes nurse, thank you, let me take that cup from your hand and watch you stand there, and wonder where it went when you awake and try to hand it to me. I like fucking with people.

A new lady is being wheeled in. She's very old, in a wheelchair. She's smoking Mores. She offers me one and tells me that her name is Betsy. I like Betsy. We hang out by the television, which I can't watch because it keeps jumping forward. She agrees with me.

"Time traveler too, huh? There's lots of us." She is like me. I don't feel as alone. Betsy is full of information. Apparently she's been here before. She really knows her way around. She won't let anybody push her wheelchair; she does it with her good foot. And she loves to give me cigarettes. There's a big pile of tobacco and papers on a countertop by the TV. "No," she says, "That will stain your fingers." I'm sitting with Betsy. She knows lots of the old people here. We're sitting in a circle, Betsy is the leader. The old people are friendlier than most of the people my age. Mores burn my throat really bad. Betsy says it's the brown paper, but once I get used to it, there's no finer taste in the world. She looks at me through her goggle glasses and says, "You're gonna be alright, kid. You are going to be just fine. Don't you worry." I think she's the first person that has said anything of the sort. Most everyone is really worried about me. Even Jimmy Simple said I was a mess. Betsy says I'm okay. I wonder if she can be my doctor. An old man who hasn't ever said a word as long as I have been here turns to me and says, "You ain't a permanent resident here, not like most of us. You're a smart kid."

If I lie on my back in my room, I can see patterns in the textured ceiling above me. It's almost time for meds, and I'm trying to figure out how to get out of taking them. They're making me very sick. I want to lie here on my back and watch the patterns change in the fresco. I see a rabbit jump and kill a dog. It's like watching clouds. Where are the clouds? If this was earth, I could see clouds. They won't let me leave here. I go ask Barbara to let me go outside for a little while and she laughs. I know that laugh. It says, "But you can't go outside in outer space, the vacuum would cause your head to implode." They have a really good painting of San Francisco out the window, and they feel that's all they need. She hands me a small glass of orange juice, and I have some. It's time to go lie down again and think about ways to get off the space ship. Maybe in a little while, I feel sleepy.

Jimmy shakes me awake. "EthanEthanEthan. They let me

go down to the commissary and buy the cigarettes. Barbara took me."

"What?"

"The gift shop in the lobby. They let me go and get the candy and the cigarettes. I got to go downstairs."

"I wanna go."

"You have to behave, and then they let you go."

Jimmy is so excited that little bits of spit are coming out of his mouth and hitting me in the face, assisted by gravity, of course, since he's leaning over me.

"Say it, don't spray it. I want the news, not the weather."

Jimmy laughs so hard he has to sit down on my bed, crushing my feet. I hit him and he scoots so that now they are no longer under his butt, but they are held hostage by the blue blanket. I think about this gift shop for a while. I didn't realize that there was one. What sort of weird outer space shit do they sell? A snowstorm on Saturn? Greetings from Mars.

Jimmy stands up, and I pull my legs out from under the covers. We're alone in the room. "Give me your hand." I grab his hand and hold the palm up to mine again. We can touch here, and no one will know or try to stop us. He is almost a foot taller than I am. He pushes me down on the bed and sits on me. It feels really nice. But then he tries to tickle me, and I writhe around under him, begging for mercy.

"Stop!@!@!" I scream. Too loud. Oops. James the head nurse runs in and yanks Jimmy off of me and leads him out of the room. We're probably both going to be punished now. Jimmy is still laughing, he thinks it was so funny. I laugh too and wait for Barbara or someone to come and sentence me to solitary confinement. No one comes. I wander out into the hall. Jimmy is in his room, lying on the bed. I poke my head into his room.

"Hey."

"Go away, don't let them see you. We have to stay separate now."

What sort of bullshit is this? Fuck these stupid people. How am I supposed to get better? What is better anyway? Betsy is holding court over by the television again. I go and sit with her. It's evening out there, or at least that's what they want me to believe.

"Hey time traveler. I'll bet you want to know what time it is right now." She digs in her bag that hangs off the side of her chair. She produces an enormous alarm clock that says Big Ben on the face. The ticking is loud and hollow, like a gun, without bullets, cocking and firing over and over again. It says 5:45. She turns it over and winds it. It wheezes like a smoker's cough.

"I see you got a little jab." She points to my arm, which is bruised where the needle went in.

"Yeah."

"Don't you wanna get out of here? Cause if you're getting jabbed like that, they're never gonna let you out of here. They reward your good behavior here, just like in grade school, sweetie."

"So you've been out before?"

"Oh yes, many many times I've gotten out of here."

"How?"

"Lots of different ways, I guess." Then, like a radio broadcast inside my ear, I hear her voice, but her mouth isn't moving.

"Take the elevator, time traveler. Just catch it."

She raises her eyebrows and winks at me. I hear the dinner cart coming down the hall, and there is the clatter of humanity preparing itself for the evening meal, served up in alien plastic. I start toward the exit door, and her voice continues on inside my head.

"Wait till the time is right, traveler. They reward you for good behavior here." I turn around, and Betsy is asleep in her wheelchair, the large clock held loosely in her lap by her long bony fingers.

Salisbury steak with mashed glue and gravy. Looks like those weird yellow squash and zucchini too. Yuck. I want some fucking pizza. I think the aliens that run this joint got all their recipes from the elementary school lunch menu. Salisbury steak, what the fuck is it? If it was hamburger, wouldn't they just call it that? What is this fucking place?

It's hatching. The plan, I mean. I'm starting to see a way out of here. But now I have to eat this chopped beef with brown cum sauce. And Jimmy isn't allowed to sit at my table. I look across the room at him, but he's busy talking some new guy out of his milk. I can't eat this shit.

CHAPTER 11

I'm good. I'm sooo good. It's arts and crafts, and I'm making a plaque, just like they want me to. I'm cutting beautiful pictures out of a magazine and gluing them to a piece of wood and painting the wood and rubbing shellac over it all. And it's looking mighty pretty. Boy, what a pretty piece of art I'm making at craft time. Yessir.

"That sure is pretty, Ethan."

"Thank you, Barbara. I'm making it for my mother. She's coming to visit later today, isn't she?"

"Yes, she is." Barbara smiles approvingly. She likes the new Ethan, the good Ethan.

"Is it time for medication yet, Barbara?"

"Not until noon."

"May I have my PRN of Cogentin, please?"

"Oh, is your neck getting stiff again?"

"Yes it is."

I've been carrying on like this for several days now. It's a miracle, they're all saying it. I'm getting better. The medicine is working. I join in all the group activities. We had a Fourth of July barbeque on the roof, and I played volleyball. The roof was interesting. It has high walls, and you can't see anything but the grey foggy sky above you. Yet another example of the huge distance that separates me from earth. Somewhere in that grey sky is my home. I'm going to get there. It's all covered in my plan.

I love having a plan. It's my secret, and nobody knows. I'll be out of here before the month is through. I've stopped telling the strangers what's inside my head. I'm just giving them what they like to hear. They like to hear please and thank you; they like to see me smile. They really like to see me organize the small pile of possessions I have on my table. I spend several minutes each morning just rearranging my razor and toothbrush. I make my bed after every nap. There are hushed whispers "it's a miracle." But every once in a while, I let something slip and they look at me disapprovingly. I'll tell an off-color joke, or burn my hand with a hand-rolled cigarette.

Here comes Jimmy. He's heading down the hallway. He doesn't really see me, he just turns around and walks away, talking to himself. Then he wheels around and heads toward me, still talking. It's not talking, it's a song. He's singing. He sees me and stops.

"Ethan, my man, what's happening?"

"What a lovely song you were just singing." Why am I bothering with him? I guess they might be observing me.

"I wrote it myself. I'm in a band, you know. Jimmy Simple and the Dead Giveaways. Have you heard of us?"

"Hmmm...no."

"We're pretty fucking obscure."

"Obviously. Who else is in the band?"

"Just me right now." He pauses, and then laughs. Then he gets a very serious look on his face.

"Ethan, come to my room, I want to talk to you."

"Oh, Jimmy, I might get in trouble." I am wearing an angel face mask while I talk to him, in case anyone is watching.

"Fuck them."

"But I'm on my best behavior."

"No one is fucking watching, come on." He grabs me by my wrist and drags me into his room, shutting the door behind him. He shares this room with two other guys, both of whom are in the television room right now. No tattle tales. I hope there aren't camera eyes anywhere.

"What's gotten into you? Why are you talking like the Beaver?"

I don't answer, not a word. My plan is secret. Only Betsy knows my plan, and I didn't even tell her because she told me. I'm holding out for that reward.

"Where'd Ethan go, huh?" He holds me by the shoulder and gently shakes me. God, some alarm somewhere is going to go off if he touches me anymore. They have sixth sense, these aliens, they can tell when two humans are relating to each other. Forbidden, against the rules, wrong. I don't want to lose all my hard earned brownie points, and this loser is going to take them all away from me. Okay, he's a nice loser. He's a cute loser, actually. I look at his face, which is rough and unfortunate. I like his face.

"What?" He wants to know why I'm looking at him. What should I tell him?

"You're sort of cute." Oh shit. That was stupid.

"Yeah, so are you." Oh great. This is going somewhere. I really don't know what we're supposed to do now. He leans toward me and holds my head in his hands. We kiss. I feel a sensation breaking through all the medicine. I'm horny. I pull away to look at Jimmy, poor guy.

Like clockwork, there's a quick knock on the door and James the head nurse comes into the room.

"Ethan, what are you doing in here? This door has to remain open at all times. You and Jimmy are officially separated, too, so why are you in here? Hmmm?"

Jimmy leaps to my defense, "I dragged him in here, James, I'm sorry. It's my fault."

"Go to your room, Ethan." Shit, I guess I should be happy at how few brownie points I just lost compared to what I might have lost if he had burst in ten seconds before. I should fucking count my goddamn blessings.

"Yessir." I obediently file out of the room and down the hall to my little bed. I don't know why, but I'm really angry. Who the fuck are these fucking assholes and why do they get to tell me what to do? I'll kiss Jimmy if I want to, and I'll hold hands with Jimmy and I'll just do whatever the fuck I please.

There's a blue plastic pitcher full of water on my bedside table. Fuck them. I pick up the pitcher and throw it as hard as I can at the window. It makes a very loud sound, and water sprays all over the room. I hear the sound of rushing feet, the sound of the thought police, coming here to tell me what I did wrong. Bastards. I am trying to please them. Now what can I do? They're still ten paces down the hall. I run to the window and bend to pick up the pitcher as they come in the room.

"Ethan, what happened?"

I put on my obsequious cow face "I am so sorry, I tried to pour myself some water, and it fell." She looks around the room. There's really no hard evidence to the contrary. True, my bed is soaked, but they can't really tell how badly. I fooled these motherfuckers.

"Okay. I'll send someone to clean up." She's serious. She fucking believed me! I turn to the mirror and give myself a high five. No one saw that either, did they? I think I'm going to get out of here really soon. I'm going to outwit them, somehow. They aren't as smart as me. As I am. Whatever.

If I can throw a pitcher and they can't figure it out, what else can I do? I can play with Jimmy's cock and they only think I'm breaking my restriction. Maybe I can start a fire with my brain. Maybe I can burn down this horrible place. I'll try that one soon. Betsy can tell me how it's done. Yeah, I'll ask Betsy. Wow, this is great. I feel great.

It's med time. I hear the squeaking wheels of the ancient rust-covered cart, filled with little plastic cups of orange juice. I hear the sound of 25 pairs of feet in foam booties shuffling across the linoleum. I hear the sound of little plastic cups being drained and tossed into the trash receptacle on the side of the cart. I hear my name being called. It's my turn to take a sip of oblivion. In a few minutes, I won't feel so great any more. I won't even remember this moment. I'll forget it all. If I try to remember this moment, can I carry it with me into the next wave of oblivion?

I'm going to bring this moment with me, and they can't have it.

I drain the cup. I throw it into the receptacle. I'm still feeling great, and I'm going to take a minute ago with me into the next ten minutes. It's my minute, not theirs. They can't read my thoughts, I'm putting up a wall of protection. It's made out of roses. There are great thorny roses around that minute of happiness. My plan is in the rosebush too. They will never know of my plan, it's mine.

My eyes are going out of focus. But inside the rosebush, everything is clear. It's clear in there, goddammit. I don't care if I can't see in there. I'm coming back to that rosebush when the medicine wears off, and I'm going to find my plan in there. I'm sleepy now.

CHAPTER 12

When I open my eyes, Wanda is there. "Hey sleepy angel. I brought you some stuff." She produces a magic wand out of a big black bag. "Here's some magic." The wand is a clear plastic tube filled with blue and silver stars that float gently in a clear Aquarian gel.

"My magic is no good here."

"We've gotta get him out of here." I know that voice. It's Sue. I can see just past Wanda, and there's Sue, and Donny is behind her. "He looks awful."

"I'm getting better." That's what I keep hearing. That's what Mom said when she was here.

"Better? What's 'better?'" Wanda wants to know.

I have to admit that I don't feel any better. Yeah, what in the fuck is better? Sue reaches past Wanda and holds my hand.

"Let's break him out of here. Let's just put him in the Rambler and go." These words are very exciting. I try to smile, but the medicine hurts my face too much.

Donny looks at me and shakes his head, "I can't believe this shit."

His familiar east coast twang makes me cry. I am crying. Donny doesn't know why, and I don't either. Wanda reaches down and lifts my head to her bosom. She hugs me while I cry into her breasts, and when I look up at her, she's crying too. From behind a mental rosebush, I remember my plan. I savor it, like salty french fries. I love my plan. I motion Wanda close to me with my finger. She leans close so I can whisper, "I have a plan. Shhh!! A way out."

"What is it, honey?" She whispers too.

"It's a plan. It goes outside. It goes back to Earth." Damn, it's fucking hard to make a sentence. "Can you take me back there, to Earth?"

"Of course. Yes. We wouldn't leave without you."

What a relief! Someone finally acknowledges that I am not on Earth. I want to tell her more, but I am afraid. "You'll take me back when I'm ready?"

"Here's my card, sweetie. Just call me collect." I get a sick feeling in my stomach thinking about the telephone. She fishes into her purse and hands me a blue card that reads, 'Wanda 2 Knight, Psychic Advisor.' "I have to go to work now, honey, I'm late. But you just call me, or here," she takes back the card and scribbles on the back, "here's my 800 number. I'm there all day long."

She picks up her enormous black bag and kisses me. "Bye Suzie, Bye Donny." She scoots out the doorway. I just told her about my plan. Why did I do that? I knew she wasn't an android, that's why. How did I know? Well, she was so human and warm. My tears would have short-circuited an android's heart.

Donny sits down beside me on the bed. "Dude, you look awful. Who cut your hair?" I reach up to my head, and there's no more long lovely locks. Just short shitty sheaves of hair.

"Is it bad?"

"Dude, it's bad."

Sue gives Donny a glare, turns to me and says, "No. You're beautiful. You're the most beautiful boy on this planet." She puts her fingers through what's left of my hair and pats my head.

"Are you getting any good drugs?" Donny looks hopeful.

"No. It's like that time. Judy."

"You mean when Judy gave us Thorazine and we had to lie down in the park for six hours?" Donny said what I was thinking. He heard my thoughts.

I nod.

"Ugh! You've got to get off this shit."

Right on cue, there is a clatter out in the hall. The cart full of orange juice comes menacingly into my room. Barbara is at the helm.

"Well, well! You sure do have a lot of visitors." She winks at me, which makes me feel sick inside. "Here you are." She extends a cup toward me with her cold robot hands.

Here you are...Here...you...are. I am not!

"That's not me!" I point to the cup. "Don't call me that!"

She doesn't follow me, but Sue does. She starts giggling. Barbara snaps at her, "What's so funny?"

Sue just keeps giggling. I take the cup, making sure that it isn't me before I drink it. I drain the cup, tasting the coppery undertaste. I wrinkle my nose. Barbara takes the cup back from me and wheels out of the room, squeaking and clattering as she goes, like a robot with loose parts.

"That stuff is bad," Sue says, "you don't need that, you need to be on a mountain somewhere, praying." I must admit that sounds like a much nicer choice. I am not orange juice, I am a mountain. I'm a hermit on a mountain.

"If you take me there, I'll stay." I mean it.

"Not now, we need a plan or something." Sue said the magic word.

"A plan? I have one!" Oh shit, I said that too loud. I've got a plan though. How can I tell them my plan without being heard. Barbara (is down the) Hall, and I'm safe.

"You get a reward here. If you're good." Sue and Donny look puzzled. My plan is easy, but I have to say it right. I can't get my words to go in the right order. They keep messing up. How am I going to tell them anything? I should just be quiet.

"Go on." Sue wants to know more.

"It's a special reward. Very special. You get the cigarettes."

Donny reaches for his backpack. "He's not making any sense, I gotta go."

"Wait!" Sue hisses. She turns to me, "What do cigarettes have to do with the mountain?"

It's a long stretch, trying to explain this. I can't get it right. I'm useless. I'll try again. "You get them. You get to get them."

"Where?" Sue seems to be catching on.

"Out that door somewhere." I point to the big blue door out in the hall. There's a big sign ten paces in front of the door that says, 'no patients beyond this point.' Donny doesn't seem interested in this plan, but Sue is very excited.

"Do you get to get them alone?"

"I don't think so. Ask Jimmy Simple. He's been." Wow, I think that made a lot of sense.

"What the fuck is he talking about?" Donny is pissed off. I guess I didn't make any sense at all.

"Shhhhhh! I'll tell you after." Sue got my psychic fax and Donny didn't. She giggles, "Who's crazy here, me or you?"

"Me." I am sure of that.

I feel a motion out in the hallway. Then I hear it. Then I see it. It's Jimmy Simple. He's very agitated. He runs into the room, and stops short when he sees Sue and Donny.

"EthanEthanEthan. Can you tell me the country code for China? I need to call China." Spit flies out of the corners of his mouth. He's a maniac. "Cool hair." He reaches out and touches Donny's hair.

"Thanks." He politely removes Jimmy's hand from his hair and puts it back at his side.

"Sue, Sue what's the country code for China?" How does he know her name? Does he know her? Is there a conspiracy against me?

"How do you know him?"

"We met him when we got here. You were asleep. We've been waiting here for an hour."

"Sue, Sue please tell me the country code for China. I've got to call China."

"I don't know. Try dialing 00 and asking her."

"Can you do it for me? Please? Donny? Will you do it?"

Donny rolls his eyes and snarls, "Dude, you're harshing my mellow. Clear out."

Jimmy misses the hostility in Donny's voice. He isn't devastated. If Donny had said that to me, in that tone, I would have cried for a week. Jimmy is too strong. He just keeps going. He mutters to himself about China and walks out of the room. I wish I was like Jimmy. Donny fishes around in his backpack and produces something very important: my journal. He hands it to me. I was writing in this when I figured out where Itt's Att. I left it on Earth. "I thought you might want this."

I am so happy I start to cry. Donny looks crestfallen, like he did the wrong thing. I have to let him know that he did right. I grab his hand.

"Thank you." I need to put my thoughts down on paper, before I drift into orange juice land. I don't have a pen, but Donny does. He gives it to me.

Donny has to go. Sue says, "Wait! You can't go and not tell him." What? I want to know what.

"I wrote it in the journal, Sue. I hate goodbyes." But he doesn't leave. He comes over to my bed and sits down beside me. He says, "Ethan, I have to leave."

"You'll come back, right?"

He shakes his head no. "Not right away. I have to go back to New Jersey."

"Why?" My lip is quivering.

"I don't have a job. They evicted us. I have to go home, Ethan." Tears are stinging my eyes. I can't quite see through them, but I can see that Donny is crying too.

"Take me with you! Please take me with you. Don't leave me here!" Donny can't answer because he's crying. He puts on his leather jacket and gives me a big sobbing hug. He pats at his eyes, which are running with eyeliner. He looks like Alice Cooper. "Read what I wrote. I'll call you." He leaves me with Sue.

"You really love him, don't you?" Sue asks. I nod between sobs. Sue has to get to work, so she goes, leaving me face down in my pillow, soaking in salty snot.

*

Dr. Sheldon Vile stares at me from across a brown desk. The edges of the desk are rubbed raw. The vinyl made to look like wood is torn, and the jaundiced pressboard shows through. He says very little. He asks me if I have any requests.

"Yes. Make me a doctor. I know where Itt's Att, so you can just give me my degree now."

He nods, and writes something in his book. "Who told you where itt's att?"

"I figured it out by myself. I talked to the phone company and they said I was right. So just give me the degree and let's get out of here."

"I'm afraid I can't do that." Bastard. Filthy bastard. He won't let me have it because he's afraid I'll be better than him. Maybe only the fucking aliens get to be doctors. I solved the puzzle, let me fucking play the real game now. I'll be damned if he gets one more word out of me. I fold my arms and stare off into space. He's heard enough. I know where Itt's Att. That's enough. He's really scribbling now. The less I say, the more he writes. I glance out the door, and I can see Betsy dragging herself by her foot along the hall. I want a smoke.

"May I go?"

"Is there anything else I can do for you? We're here to help you, Ethan."

"No." I push my chair back, shake his hand and leave. I catch sight of Betsy just as she pulls into the entrance to the TV room. I run after her. "Betsy! Got any smokes?"

"Sure, Ethan." She smiles at me through her coke bottle lenses. "I always have a smoke for a young handsome lad such as yourself." She pulls out a long brown More cigarette and hands it to me. She fishes in her side saddlebag and produces a yellow disposable lighter. After two tries, she gets it to stay and I light my cigarette. "Getting low. Cigarettes I mean."

"Where do you get them from?"

"You know, sweetie. They let the good ones go down and get them." She winks her incredibly magnified eye at me. She knows.

"How long till they let me go?"

"You gotta stop talking nonsense. Nobody cares where Itt's Att, doll. Just tell them about your meals and your meds and don't let on that anything else is going on in that fool head of yours."

"You're good. I can't even tell what's wrong with you. Why don't they let you go, Betsy?"

She puffs hard, like a dragon. Smoke billows from her mouth.

"They don't let the old and feeble go. We're just allowed to spend. We can't go shopping." There is really no reason why she should be here. Maybe she's my guardian angel, sent to protect me.

"Yes." She heard my thoughts. Did she say that, or did I think it? Betsy is an angel. She has wheels for wings. Her hair hasn't been washed in a long time. It's sort of matted to her head. There are craters on her face, too. Angels come in disguise, like the story of the Buddha that appeared to a pilgrim as a dead dog. I kiss her on the cheek, right where a bad blemish festers, and she pats my shoulder. "You're a good soul." So she says.

*

Jimmy runs up and down the hallway, banking his invisible skateboard, and grinding his blank wheels on an imagined coping. He holds onto the see-thru board as he leaps over small pieces of furniture idling in the hallway. There is no one around to stop him. It's random moments like these that make life here seem almost bearable. My head still feels like they took out my brain and stuffed it with cotton. There's even sort of a raw achy feeling up there. Almost everyone has gone upstairs to the volleyball game. I got excused because I had the appointment with Dr. Vile. Betsy can't play, so they don't even try to make her. Jimmy can weasel his way out of anything. He stops skateboarding and comes over to where I am sitting, watching him. He sits next to me and puts his arm around my shoulders, hugging me close to him.

"Quit it, we could get in trouble." He just looks into my eyes and says nothing. I feel really uncomfortable being this close to him. He's weird. His arm is holding me at an awkward angle, and it would be very hard to break out of this hold. I feel claustrophobic. His breath smells faintly of onions. His eyes are heavy lidded from the medication.

"Ethan, will you come live with me?"

"No."

"Yes, you will." He smiles. I don't have a lot of options right now, so I will consider this one. "I've got a cool place."

"Go on." I'm sort of curious.

"I have this apartment in the Mission, and SSI pays for it. It's called section 8. I get really lonely there. Why don't you come live with me there?"

"How are we going to get to San Francisco from here?"

"You don't still think we're on a space station, do you?"

"Prove it. Prove that we're not." I look at him with a wild stare. He shrugs. James the head nurse rounds the bend and sees us in our strange embrace.

"You know the rules, Ethan. No touching." He is a retard. Can't he see that Jimmy's the one touching me? I hate this place. Jimmy doesn't let go of me, he just holds me defiantly. James keeps walking, never thinking for even one second that we might have defied him and held on. Fuck him. I hold Jimmy's hand, flouting all authority. I stick my tongue out at James' back as he rounds the next corner, oblivious.

Jimmy continues, "It's kinda small, but there's a hot plate

so I can cook for you and I have a bunk bed. You can have the top bunk if you want it. And I have one of those square refrigerators. It needs cleaning, maybe you can do that. And then I have a television. Oh yeah you don't like television. My coffee maker broke...well, I broke it. But I stole an electric teakettle from Westside Lodge, so I drink instant--"

"Jimmy, you don't need coffee."

"Will you come live with me, Ethan? Please?"

"I have to think about it."

Jimmy's face turns into a scowl. He pushes me away from him, and goes back to his skateboarding sans board. Maybe I should have just said yes. Now he's mad at me. Or maybe his attention span ran out.

I shuffle back to my room. It hurts to lift my feet up. Scuff Scuff Scuff. My little foam hospital booties slide well on these concrete floors. Scuff Scuff Scuff. I'm at my bed now. As I start to lie down, I notice that there's a book on my nightstand. It's my journal. What's inside? I open it up. It randomly opens to my birthday from this year. How weird.

"2-27-87: The world can be the world sometimes. I need violent energy because I am. I see the sense I don't make. I see the skinhead I wish to lay." Oh yeah, there was a cute skinhead at my birthday party this year. I flip the pages and land on an entry from early June. "6-4-87: Name for a Band, Liquid Eyeliner with Wanda." Two days later, "6-6-87 Art is born out of anarchy. Anarchy is born out of credit. Anarchy is best left in the hands of the very well educated to lead this new 4th caste of homeless anarchists to triumph over the un-united 'true crazies' who are too weak to overpower the forces that tear at their modern lives. Anarchists must become self-dependent to achieve harmony in a caste system." Whatever. Then my eye catches sight of some familiar handwriting. It's Donny. He wrote in my journal.

"7-2-87: Ethan- it's time to redeem myself to those who love me for putting them thru undeserving grief and heartache and it's time for me to make them proud of me. I'm still young I can't fuck up again. I've gotten all the bitterness and anger and resentment toward society out of my system and I'm ready to start living and I've realized that you have to pay for everything (karma). That for every decadent pleasure I've gotten out of life I've had to pay for because I had a tense-karma lifestyle and I can basically live the way I've been living (with a few obvious changes) and try. TRY. Try to do something to promote my life instead of existing in a constant state of trying to escape. You've helped me, supported me. We've both helped each other and learned from each other and in return we've both received something priceless: an eternal friend. Somebody that will always help you as much as I can. I will miss you." I can't see very well, and the paper is warping in tear-soaked bumps.

CHAPTER 13

I'm so excited, I can hardly breathe. They just told me that I can go get the cigarettes this afternoon. What time is it? It's 11:30. I get to go get the cigarettes and candy bars at 1 p.m. Looking over my shoulder the whole time, I approach the pay phone in the hallway. I can taste a cold metal taste in the back of my throat. That's fear. I start shaking as I retrieve Wanda's card from my journal and dial her 800-number. The operator's voice comes on. I hope she won't be listening. Oh, it's the automated attendant. I dial Wanda's extension. Wanda answers.

"Great American Trading Company. This is Wanda. Can I help you?"

"Wanda, it's me. Ethan."

Ethie!!!" She squeals so loud, that a man standing nearby looks over at me. He heard her.

"Shhhh! The plan. It's ready."

"What plan?" She forgot!!

"I get to go get the cigarettes, just like I told Sue."

"OH. Are you going to make a break for it?"

I glance over my shoulder. There must be wire taps on this fucking thing. How can I do this? I guess I should just pretend there aren't. If there aren't, my plan will work. If there are, it will fail. It's just that simple. It's a fucking Schroedinger Cat.

"Yeah. I'm going at 1 this afternoon. Will you be there?"

"I'll try. Sue's got to bring the car. I tell you what, why don't you meet us outside the hospital?"

"Where?"

"Uh, we'll be at 22nd and Potrero. You have to make a run for it." I nod, until I realize she can't hear me nodding.

"Oh. Which way is that?"

"Right, sorry. I forget you didn't exactly walk in there by yourself. If you leave out the main doors, it's straight ahead until you reach the busy street. That's Potrero. Then you make a right and scurry down about one block to 22nd street. Are you wearing that ugly chartreuse smock?"

I look down. I am wearing a green smock. "Yeah."

"Didn't your dad leave you some nice clothes?"

Come to think of it, there are some really tacky shirts in my little cabinet. "I don't know if it was him."

"It was. I met him. He seemed very sweet."

"I guess he is. I don't really know."

"Wear that, and those jeans that Donny brought you. That way you'll look normal."

Wow, she's really helping with my plan. "Okay. See you at 1 o'clock."

This is it. I'm getting out. In my room, I open the cabinet and take out one of the shirts. It's maroon, with a little blue polo player on the left breast pocket. It's really embarrassing to me to have to wear it. I yearn for those piles of clothing back in the tenderloin. Where are they now?

In the mirror, I look like a preppy. I have on black jeans

and my hair, what's left of it, is combed. I am very excited to be leaving. It took me almost half an hour to tie my shoes. I just couldn't get my fingers to do the knots. And the buttons on this shirt were stiff. It really hurt putting it on. The fabric is new, and my skin is sore to the touch. I don't feel comfortable at all. Like a preppy. I can't find my electric razor. Someone took it. My face hurts when I smile because all the little sharp hairs at the edge of my mouth keep poking me. Something is poking me in the side. It's one of the pins that held the shirt in its folded form. I must have missed it. Barbara is at the door.

"You ready, Ethan?" She is all smiles.

"Yep."

"Look at you, all dressed. I haven't seen you in anything but a gown since you got here. You're a handsome boy. You should dress this way more often."

She takes my hand as she chatters at me. She leads me past the sign that reads "no patients past this point." I don't vaporize. She wears a key around her neck, which she takes and puts in a metal box by the door. A light above the door flashes red, then green. The door makes a click. She opens it. There are aliens dressed as nurses and doctors coming and going out in the hall. Some of them rush past us, nearly knocking me down. Whew! It's busy out here. Barbara holds onto my hand very tightly. It's not going to be easy. We arrive at an elevator. Barbara pushes the down button and waits. She smiles at me again, and hands me an envelope from her pocket.

"Here's the money. You get to buy it."

I look at the envelope incredulously. Money! Inside, there are a great many paper bills, almost all ones, a dozen quarters, and about fifty dimes, nickels and pennies. This money comes directly from the patients. It's not hospital money, no. It's patient money. And here I am holding it. The elevator doors swing open and we step inside. There are other people in the elevator with us. They don't seem to notice that I am not one of them. I am already blending in with this world. The metal taste by my tonsils is so intense I start to wonder if I've got a bullet lodged back there. My stomach hurts. Panic is setting in and getting the better of me. How in the fuck am I going to do this?

The light on the elevator reads 3, 2, L. The doors open, and everyone pushes to get out. I stumble forward. Barbara's still got her hand on mine. The envelope comes loose from my other hand and the contents spill out into the hallway. Money flies everywhere. Barabara panics, and lets go of my hand. I scream very loudly, "WAAAAAAAAHHHH!" And then I take off running.

There are people everywhere. Screaming was supposed to make everyone confused. I thought if I screamed, I would create a sort of smokescreen. No. Everyone is looking at me as I run past them. I have to hurdle right over an old man in a wheelchair who blocks my path to the door. I see the gift shop, and the doors beyond. Oh no. There's a guard in the gift shop, and he's just dropped his coffee. He spilled it all down the front of his uniform. He's wiping it off of himself as I speed past him. He lifts a walkie-talkie to his mouth. It will be better if I don't look behind me.

The doors are automatic. I nearly plow into them, I'm running so fast. But they swing open and I rush past. I smell the air. It smells good. I am in San Francisco. There's no fucking spaceship. Why the fuck didn't they just let me come down here? Behind the wheel of a yellow Oldsmobile is an extremely old person of indeterminate gender. Driving as many old people do, he or she drives slowly but without regard to the surroundings. My planned trajectory will place me in the path of this slow moving but deadly beast. I must make a quick decision, to angle to the left and go behind her, or to the right and try to make the cut in front of her. The right is closer to my destination at 22nd street and Potrero, but the left seems safer. I hear a fat security guard behind me, so I am forced to choose the more dangerous path to the right. This will double my odds of making it if I am not struck by the car, for he will be cut off by the octogenarian menace and be forced to veer around to the left, or perhaps wait until the path is cleared. All this fresh air is making my mind work. I angle sharply to the right, keeping my eyes focused on the flower patch that lies just to the other side of this road. I feel like all those months of playing Frogger on the Atari have finally paid off. I will make it across. The old person sees me and raises his or her hands in horror. I hear the squeal of brakes as the bright yellow nose of the Oldsmobile plows toward me. This is a driveway, you fool; you should expect patients to come running past you. The car slows and stops, blocking the security guard, I hope. I have not looked behind me. I am trampling through the lavender. My foot lands on an unexpected sprinkler head, twisting my ankle and sending jolts of pain through my body.

The shoes were a good idea. There is a lot of rough terrain here, and I would have been slowed down quite a bit if I were in my foam booties. I sense pain messages coming from down by my ankle, but I close my head to them, focused on the adrenaline rush and the promise of freedom that lies at the next corner. Potrero is a very busy street. I am glad Wanda hadn't planned for me to cross it. I turn right and sprint down the sidewalk. I haven't had to run like this in a while. I feel my mind entering my body, giving it orders like a drill sergeant. The muscles are tight, but they long to do their job again, after I don't know how many weeks of unemployment. There are no streets to cross between here and 22nd street. The sidewalk is free of obstacles and there are no pedestrians. This is an excellent chance to steal a glance behind me, and size up the degree of distance between me and captivity.

Maybe it wasn't such a good idea to look back. I see the security guard is really only a few yards behind me, and he is gaining on me. I'm out of shape, and his job is on the line. I look ahead again. My eyesight hasn't been too good, thanks to the medicine, but I can make out a murky shape at the corner that looks like Sue's Duster. It is. And there's a big blond shape that must be Wanda. I'm getting closer, but I can almost feel that security guard breathing down my neck. I feel a meaty paw come out and grab at me, missing. There is a high iron fence that surrounds the perimeter of the hospital. I can see through it, where another security guard is keeping pace with me on the outside. How is he going to scale the fence? I've got nothing to worry about. Except that there is a double row of concrete pillars up ahead that looks an awful lot like a gate, even from this angle. It is, it's a gate. And he's running for the gate, to intercept me. I can see Wanda's face now. She's not smiling. She is stepping back into the car. The fat officer is winded, he's lost some ground. All that stands between me and the Duster ride to freedom is this new assailant on the other side of the fence. He's reached the fence, and the gate swings open. He's in front of me. I can try to make it past him, but I think he's ready for that. I have to do something unpredictable. Sue starts the Duster, I hear the engine roar to life. How will I make it to that car? I don't want the guards to see Wanda or Sue, or else there will be trouble.

There's very little I can do right now. I can run out into traffic, and take the chance of being plowed down by a number 47 bus. I can turn around and take my chances with the fat security guard, but then the new one, who seems pretty muscular, is going to get me. Actually as I look at the new one, I realize he's really hot. He's Hispanic, and his arms are bulging with muscle. I also remember that the original purpose of this excursion was to get a ride back to Earth with Sue and Wanda, but by all the signs it seems that I am already back on Earth. So in a way, I've already got my ride. I'm home. The Hispanic guard is dressed differently from the other one. He's a police officer.

He stands like a football player, hunched over, waiting for me to break in his direction. The security guard behind me has come to a stop, unable to continue. All I can think is how nice it's going to feel to have his big arms around me. I throw open my arms wide and come to a stop about three paces in front of him. He runs for me, throwing his huge arms around me and tackling me. I don't resist. My body falls flat and my head smashes into the sidewalk. He has me pinned at the waist, but my shoulders are free.

Through little tiny flashes of light I can see his sweaty brow and the angry eyes that glare at me. Past his meaty arms I see Sue's Duster driving away, avoiding trouble. I gaze at the police officer's mouth, curled in a snarl. I see his badge which reads "Oro en paz, hierro en guerra." I reach up and kiss him on the lips, and the lights go out.

CHAPTER 14

When I open my eyes, there's my mother. She's sitting on a chair against the wall, crying into her book. She doesn't see my eyes open. Good. I close them tight and try to go back to sleep. No good. I can keep my eyes closed but the consciousness won't go away. I push really hard, and blood courses through the blood vessels in my brain. I hear it in my ears; I can feel pressure mounting behind my eyes. It doesn't make me sleepy, it just gives me a big headache. I move my head slightly and hear a crinkling noise like disposable diapers. It must be a bandage on the back of my head. Oh damn, my head hurts! It hurts to move my eyes behind the closed lids.

My nose itches, so I scratch it. I hear the sound of my mother's chair scooching against the hard cement floor. My mother rushes to the side of my bed. I can smell her and feel the breeze she generated. I hear her breathing.

"Ethan, Ethan honey? Can you hear me?" Shit, I blew it. I open one eye cautiously. She's smiling at me through tears. I close my eye again, vainly hoping that she'll vanish. Plenty of other shit here has been a figment of my imagination, so why not her?

"Nurse! Nurse! He's awake!" Goddammit, I am not imagining that shrill voice. I give in and open both of my eyes. She's still there, quaking with tears of relief. "Ethan, honey, can you hear me?" I nod, which hurts a lot and makes the sound of a diaper clad baby wiggling its butt. "Are you feeling okay?"

"Yeah." Talking hurts less.

Her face contorts into a snarl. "Good. How about telling me just what the fuck you thought you were doing today? What kind of stunt did you try to pull? Huh?" She's furious. I close my eyes, pretending to lapse into unconsciousness. She doesn't buy it. "Don't pull that bullshit with me! Open your goddamn eyes!"

"Hey, what's going on here?" I hear Barbara Hall's voice as she enters the room.

"Open your eyes, before I slap you...He was awake a minute ago, I swear...Ethan!" I keep my eyes shut. It's the only thing I can do.

Barabara intercepts her, "Why don't we just let him--"

"Keep your fucking hands off of me!"

"Ma'am, I'm going to have to ask you to leave if you continue like this." Barbara is laying down the law; I love it.

"Fine!" Mom storms out of the room.

Barbara comes to my bedside. I feel her maternal hand brush back my hair. I open one eye again. She smiles at me and winks. I can see the coast is clear, I open the other eye.

"Well, you had quite an adventure today, didn't you?" She's all smiles, no hostility.

I grin sheepishly. "I'm sorry."

"Don't apologize to me. I didn't get hurt, you did."

"I guess I'll never get out of here now."

She smiles, genuinely. "When you get better."

"I made it, though."

"Where?" She leans closer to me.

"Home."

"So are we off the spaceship yet?"

"Barbara, it wasn't a spaceship, it was a hospital. Still is."

She smiles broadly at me. "We're in a hospital. Do you still care where it's at?"

"I know where itt's att."

"Uh oh. Where's it at?" She looks worried.

"San Francisco."

"Yes." She's really smiling now.

"If you had only let me out, even for one minute, I could have seen for myself."

She looks pensive. She takes my hand and holds it. "You are probably right. It just isn't set up that way."

Dr. Vile enters the room and clears his throat. Barbara backs away, letting my hand drop to my side. Dr Vile leans in and looks me in the eyes. He holds up a finger in front of my face. "How many fingers do you see."

"Four, plus your thumb."

He clears his throat rather abruptly. "How many am I holding up?"

"One."

"Good. Now follow the finger." He moves the finger around and I follow it with my eyes, as he requested. "Good. Any headache?"

"Yes."

"Nausea?"

"No."

"A mild concussion. You'll be just fine." He turns to leave.

"Wait, Doctor."

"What is it?"

"Where's my mother?"

"She's not here anymore, thank God. I suspect she went home, to leave us all in peace. Awfully kind of her."

"Home to Vermont?"

"No, we're not that lucky." He hurries out the door, his white lab jacket flapping behind him. Barbara comes back to my bedside and smoothes my hair down against my forehead.

"I don't know how you survived this long with her." She means it. I guess my mother is pretty dangerous, really. "Why don't you get some rest. That officer gave you a good knock. You need to sleep it off."

I can't sleep. Barbara leaves. There's a container of pudding by my bed. I reach over and get it, taking care not to move my head too much. The pudding is tightly sealed with foil. As I struggle to remove the foil, my head starts to throb. The foil gives way, and the top is off. There's a gob of tapioca stuck to the foil. I lick it off. It tastes delicious. It's earth tapioca, not space tapioca. I am so glad to be eating it. I don't have a spoon, so I lick the tapioca from the container. At first it's easy. But now the tapioca is deeper in the cup, and I have to put my nose in there, like a dog. I get tapioca all over the top of my nose. I don't care. It's fucking delicious, I don't care.

Jimmy Simple fills the doorframe. He tumbles into the room,

wide eyed. "Ethan, dude. You broke out. Give me five." He holds up his massive paw, and I reach up and whack it with my tiny hand. "Everyone is talking about you."

I roll my eyes. "Let them say what they want. I'll pay them back when I get the money."

"No, man. I mean like you're their hero."

"What? I get creamed by a cop, and I'm a hero?"

"Yeah. You tried to get away. You broke the rules. Of course you're a fucking hero. I think you're a hero."

"Thanks. This hero has a headache right now." I turn to the light beside me, forgetting how my head has a sore diaper in the back. Squish, crinkle. Fuck that hurts. I reach for the light, but Jimmy beats me to it, flicking it off.

"I bet. Rest up." He zooms out of the room as fast as he came. I'm noticing something refreshing here. I don't seem to be experiencing as many of those time lapses as I used to. This is good. It's beginning to feel like life again up here in my head. I wish there was a television in this room. I feel like watching the World Wrestling Federation right about now. Maybe not, I'm feeling a little sleepy.

*

Sue is standing there when I wake up. "Ethan, what did you tell them about the plan?"

"Nothing."

"Good. It would be better if you didn't say anything." Of

course not. What they don't know won't hurt them. She reaches forward and brushes the hair out of my eyes. "You've got two black eyes...look. I'm sorry we didn't get you out of here."

"You brought me home." Sue sighs and a tear rolls out of her eye and down her chubby cheek.

"You're home?" she asks me.

"Yep."

"Good. Where were you?"

"I was on a spaceship, I think. At least part of the time."

Sue looks at me squarely and says, "If anyone else asks you, don't you dare say that. You just weren't feeling well. Got it?"

"Yes." I lie. How will I remember it? They took all my brains out and put cotton up there. I've got no memory.

"Do you care where itt's att?"

"I know where itt's att."

"Well stuff it. Don't tell these goddamn nurses here. They don't understand what you're trying to tell them. But I do. So just keep it between us, okay?"

I nod, wincing. My head still sounds like a mewling infant in disposable diapers. And it's starting to kick, too.

"Oh baby. Does it hurt?" There are more tears in her eyes as she leans forward and kisses me on the head. I reach out and grab her hand, looking into her eyes. Her lower lip is quivering. She looks back into my eyes, and I can't help but cry a little myself. She tries to smile, but more tears come and she lets out a little sob.

She cries, "I want my Ethie back."

"Me too." Where did I go? How do I get back?

She reaches forward and kisses me on the head again. I don't know why, but I reach up and touch her chin, motioning her down to my lips. When she bends down and kisses me on the mouth, I put my tongue in her mouth. She frenches me back, and her eyes open really wide, a giggle escaping even as our lips are locked, air blowing out around our lips. She puts one hand on my cheeks and closes her eyes as she kisses me. What the fuck am I doing?

I quickly pull away and look to the side of the room. My head is swimming. No touching. It feels like a little squirrel is up there, running on a wheel. My face is hot. Sue can see my reaction and she looks worried. I don't feel well.

"Sue, I need to lay down. My head hurts."

"Fine. I'll be back." She turns and leaves the room with just enough deliberation to seem offended. I am worried now because I kissed her. What was I thinking? Or not thinking? My head is all swollen, and the pressure against the pillow is making me feel nauseated. Time to close my eyes.

*

There's a round man in my room, with wire-rimmed spectacles across a moon shaped face. He looks into my eyes as he speaks to me:

"Northeast Lodge is close to your old job at the Stud." He looks like a whole bunch of perfectly drawn circles. For some reason he makes me think of the Spirograph set I had as a kid. I think that was mine. Maybe not. His glasses especially make me think of the ridged plastic, almost sharp at the edges. I used to try to wedge my finger between the sharp ridges and the inner circle, pretending it was a grindstone. "...good place for you?" There's a hint of question in what he asks, I just wasn't paying attention. I'll go for honesty.

"Could you repeat the question, I didn't hear you." He rolls his round eyes inside of their little round cages and looks over at Barbara. She nods.

"Do you think that Northeast Lodge would be a place you are interested in moving to?" What the hell do I know. It's near the Stud, he just said that. Sounds fine.

"Sounds fine."

"Great. Let me give you my card." He digs into his satchel and produces a card with a little round man made of circles drawn on it. How funny, he must know he's round. It says, "David Gates, Director. Northeast Lodge. 272 9th Street. San Francisco, CA 94103." He reaches forward to shake my hand. As I lean forward to reciprocate, I feel the familiar crinkle of the bandage. Some of the tape is stuck to the pillow, and as it separates, it sends little shockwaves of pain down my spine.

"Please please, stay there." He reaches forward and pushes me back into the pillow, taking my hand and gently shaking it in his puffy round palm. He seems like he could get me out of here; he has that kind of power. I think I'd better let him know what I know.

"I know where itt's att."

"Oh yes well of course, it's right by the Stud, where you used to work."

"No, I know--"

Barbara interrupts, "Yep, we've all been by there." She turns to me with a smile which turns into a little dagger throwing stare. David the Round Man doesn't even notice.

I have to let him know something. "See you round." I say it with special emphasis on the 'round.' There is a faint glimmer in his eye as he turns to me and says, "Yes, you will."

Has he read my mind? He is telling me that I get to leave the hospital. I love this double entendre game. Barbara is far too dimwitted to notice anything here.

"There's a Nor'easter blowing," I say.

"Ho ho. Yes." He turns away quickly and waddles out of the room. The game was just starting to get fun. Oh well, he said that I'll see him round, and that means more than one thing. I'll play it again the next time I see him. Barbara follows him out into the hallway, where they speak in hushed tones.

Jimmy Simple bounds into the room. "EthanEthanEthan"

He is so excited. "Ethan, guess what?"

"What?"

"They're letting me go today. I get to go home."

Before I even know they're there, my eyes are flooded with tears. I tear my bandaged head away from the pillow to lean forward and sob into my hands. Jimmy grabs me and holds me in his arms. My head hurts terribly, but it feels good to be held. Barbara pokes her head into the room.

"No touching." Then she pokes her head right back out again. I guess she's not going to stick around to enforce it.

"Don't cry, Ethan. You'll get out of here."

"Why--why is everyone--leaving?" It comes out between sobs.

Jimmy breaks away and starts dancing around the bed.

"Crybaby crybaby, Ethan is a crybaby. Hah!" I think he wants me to laugh, but I'm just not feeling up to it. My head feels like shit. My hands are snotty and wet. "I'm sorry, Ethan, I didn't mean it." He comes back over and holds me against his chest. I can hear his heart beating in there. It doesn't hurt so bad when my head is up against him. His chest is soft and warm. I just let it all out. I cry because my father left when I was five. I cry because Donny's gone. I cry because I don't remember who I am. I cry because I kissed Sue and didn't mean it. I cry because Jimmy won't be here tomorrow to hold my head against him. I won't hear his heart beat tomorrow.

"Hey! Tsk!" It's Barbara. She comes over and pries Jimmy away from me. He gets a violent look in his eyes for a second. Then he just sits still. He wants to leave more than he wants to fight. "You could hurt him. He has a head injury. Get on back to your room." She turns to me, "Are you okay?"

I nod, even though it hurts more than saying "yeah." If I make any noise out of my mouth I'll start sobbing. The tears flow in streams down my nose and into the corners of my mouth and off my chin into my lap.

"You're sad because your friend is leaving?"

More painful nods.

"That's good, because it means you're getting better. Just think, last week you wouldn't remember he was leaving by now, would you?"

The tears just keep coming. What the fuck is wrong with me that I need to be worried about getting better? Wasn't I just graduating with honors from high school a few months ago? Who am I? I was straight A's and now I'm barely able to remember if I'm wearing shoes or holding a pitcher of water. I'm a failure. A dropout. That's what I am. Mom calls me that. Failure. Faggot. Failure. My life is in the gutter. Barbara holds me near to her. She's breaking the no touching rule for me. Her body doesn't feel as warm as Jimmy's. His skin was really tight and hers is kind of loose. But you know what? I'm just not in the mood to turn this shit down. I need something, anything right now. I hold Barbara and shake off the tears. They're losing their grip. I'm coming back out of the well. She runs her fingers through my hair, dislodging a few stray hairs from the bandage or my scalp, whichever holds tightest.

CHAPTER 15

The day room is filled almost to capacity. It's a Giants game. Who gives a flying fuck about baseball? Not Betsy. She sits and smokes while I sit in a hard plastic chair beside her. She doesn't say much, just keeps looking at me and then looking away.

"Your eyes are getting better. The purple is fading." I don't know for sure that she actually said that. I heard it, but she may not have said it. That's how she is. She can say complete sentences without speaking. I think it's a little weird.

"It's not weird, it's just who we are, boy." There she goes again. I will never get out of here if I try to tell anybody about this. "I hate baseball too." She is really on a roll this afternoon. I feel like Danny in The Shining. She's shining me. I think I need to close my head up and keep her out for a little while, because I'm trying to get better.

"Suit yourself." And she's gone, out of my head as quick as she came. She blows out some smoke rings, turns to me, and smiles. I reach up and poke my finger through two of the rings.

*

They took my bandage off today. There's a really funky spot on the back of my head where it's crusty and little short hairs are coming in from where they shaved and gave me stitches. The bandage had that iodine smell in it. I love that smell. I wish there was a fragrance called "Hospital." It would smell like iodine and paper tape and gauze. They took my bandage off today, and I remembered it.

*

It must be two in the morning. It's pitch dark outside, but inside, the fluorescent bulbs light the hallways in pale green. There are shouts and thumps coming from the entryway. I tiptoe to the doorway, to see the orderlies wrestling a newcomer into the facility. They've got a live one. The black guy has the new guy in a headlock, so I can't see his face, but he's kicking. Then he yells, "Let me go goddammit!" I know that voice: it's Jimmy Simple. They hustle him down the hallway into one of those rooms with the tables with leather straps. They're going to restrain him. Jimmy's back.

*

The sun is up. I rush down the hallway to that room and there's Jimmy, lying on his back, looking at the ceiling. He doesn't see me. I nudge the door open, and he lifts his head, weakly smiling. "Hey, Ethan."

"Hi Jimmy. You're back."

"Yeah, I forgot my comb so I figured I'd just come back and get it." He chuckles weakly. I can tell they have him really doped up. I risk a little trouble from the nurses and let the door swing shut behind me, approaching the restraining table. Jimmy puts his arm up as far as it will go. "Can I get a hug?"

I spread my arms wide and lift his body to mine, hugging him tightly. I feel him shaking. He's crying. I stay in the embrace, holding his head to my heart. He cries like a baby, whining and sobbing. I really don't know what to say.

"I love you Jimmy."

He sniffs and breaks out of it a little. "I love you too, man." He squeezes my arms and lies back down on the table. "It's just one big fucking circle." Tears run silently down his cheeks and into his ears. He looks at the ceiling, mumbling to himself. I tiptoe back out of the room.

CHAPTER 16

I didn't think it was going to be this simple. They told me I was going to have to fill out an application for Northeast Lodge. I was dreading it from the moment I heard about it. I pictured it full of essay questions, number two pencil bubbles, the works. It's one piece of paper. It asks for my name, my date of birth, social security number. Easy. The "essay question" (and there's only one) reads: "How do you think you could benefit from your stay at Northeast Lodge?" Most of the rest of the page says "For Office Use Only." I can sum it up in one sentence: "It sounds like a nice place to rest up and get better." For a minute I worry that I might get rejected based on that answer. I show it to Barbara, and she smiles in a most condescending way and says, "Perfect, Ethan. What a lovely job you've done filling this out." And I never see it again. She takes it in to the doctor and that's that.

*

A man from the Social Security Administration comes to talk to me and take down my information. He wants to know all the places I've worked:

The Union Cafe

Marriott's Great America

Second Coming Records

The Milk Bar

The Stud

Then he wants to know where my mother was born

Brooklyn

Then he wants to know who my primary caregiver is:

Me

Do I have difficulties completing tasks that used to be no problem for me?

Yes

Please give me some examples

Tying my shoes

Shaving

Dancing

Have I been unable to work for any length of time because of my disability?

Yes. I lost my job at the Stud because I went crazy.

Describe your daily activities

I wake up, shower (sometimes), smoke, eat, smoke, go to meeting or group art, smoke, eat, smoke, try to shave and/or brush my teeth, watch TV, eat, take an Ativan, smoke, lie down and wait to fall asleep.

Do you have any hobbies?

Witchcraft and UFOlogy

How often do you watch television?

Once or twice a day

What shows do you typically watch?

Bewitched and I Dream of Jeanie. Anything magical.

Do you have difficulty following instructions?

I forget as soon as they tell me.

He is sort of cute, and he laughs at a lot of the things I say in a way which means he likes me. I like him too. I guess if this was a different situation, where I wasn't an inmate at an asylum and he wasn't a licensed social worker, then maybe I could ask him out. Oh well. The medicine they're giving me is too strong and I can't get it up much anyway. Who wants to go on a date with a limp-dicked psychotic?

*

Barbara told me that my discharge date is one week from today! I got accepted at Northeast Lodge! I'm going to get out of here! She says it will be two to three months before I hear whether or not I get SSI. They said I haven't worked enough to get social security. I don't know what that means. Jimmy is happy for me. He brought me some photos of him on his skateboard. He said his mother took them because he doesn't have any friends. He looks really happy when he's catching air. That's why he had to run up and down the halls pretending to be on his board. He needs to be happy.

The medicine they're giving me is so awful. Every time I take it, it makes me dizzy and tired. It's called "Prolixin." Barbara says it comes from the Latin Prolix, meaning abundance. Abundance of pain, discomfort, and nausea, I say. Last night I had a dream that I was three years old again. My father held my hand, and I was very happy. In a crowded room, a dog tried to bite my butt. I started to cry, and my father picked me up in his arms and held me there, tightly, until I stopped crying and then I started playing with his beard. Everyone in the room smiled at me and I felt like I belonged there. It stung hard to wake up from that. It hurt to come back to this reality, where there's no one to pick me up and hold me tightly, and where I feel the abundance of unwanted sensations that Prolixin has to offer me. I want to sleep all the time now, because my dreams are the only place this medicine can't get to, where I feel like I belong again. I hate being alive. I hope we still dream when we're dead.

CHAPTER 17

Sunlight is pouring into my room. The summer fog didn't come today. The nurses complained that it was hot outside. In here, it's still just a balmy 71 degrees, as always. Nothing changes in here. There is no outside in here. The weather is just a vague phenomenon outside the window. The window won't open, so I can only place my hand against the glass. Sure enough, there is heat beyond this window; the glass is warm to the touch. I can see the sun. The ultraviolet rays can't penetrate this glass. If I was an iguana, it would be deadly for me to stay here. My bones would dissolve into rubber and my mouth would hang open. Eventually my bones would break and my parietal eye would go blind. How good can it be for a human to be deprived of sunlight?

"Not very." I turn around but no one is there. A moment later Betsy rolls quickly past my door. I guess I don't hate it when she does that.

"Better not," she replies from halfway down the hall.

In less than a week I'll be out of here. I'll stand in the sun and feel the breeze on my cheek. How long have I been in this shit hole? I think the last thing I remember it was June. Now it must be July or even August. What day is it? My internal clock, which was out of order for quite a while, seems to be working again. I'll go test it. I think it's three o'clock.

"Barbara, what time is it?"

"It's two-forty."

"And what day is it?"

"It's Wednesday." She didn't understand my question

"I mean what month, what day?"

"Wednesday, July 29th." I'm glad she knew that, but I still don't know how long I've been in this place.

"So, when did I get here?"

"I think it was June 8th or so." She is busy, another patient is tugging on her arm. She snaps at them, "no touching."

So I've been here almost two months. Two months of my life just vanished like sand from a broken hourglass. "Thanks."

Back in my room, I stand at the window and look at the sky. Let me see if I can remember what happened in these two months. I remember my father, but I'm not sure if he was really here. I sort of wish my mother hadn't come, but I think she did. I'm really embarrassed by her. She always makes a stink about stuff. I think there were some art classes and a few meetings with doctors. I vaguely remember them putting me in a big machine to look at my head and they told me that there were no organic complications. And I wanted them to make me a doctor so I asked but they refused. It seems like a silly request now. Wanda came and Sue and they wanted to take me away from here but the cops came, and one knocked me to the ground. That's how I got the diaper-sized bandage on the back of my head. Jimmy Simple left but they dragged him back. That accounts for a few hours of the last two months. Where did the rest go? As if in answer to my question, my eye catches the little night stand by my bed. There lies my journal. I don't remember writing in it, but I have to check just in case.

I'm horrified to discover that I did write in there. I seemed to know the dates, and I even made sense in a few places. A lot of it is scribbles and drawings and diagrams of ideas that made much more sense to me at the time I drew them. I drew a cross section of my head with a star of David where the brain should be. I wrote "Pie Sees Stein."

There are a number of places where the words come together in crosses:

```
        S
        E
        C
    A R Y A N
        E
      S T A T E
```

And lots of doodles that mean nothing to me. Since I was in such a different head space, I'm not really surprised by the nonsense. What really scares me is the stuff I wrote that almost makes sense, but not quite like a letter to Donny that I wrote:

June 19
Dear Donny,
Allow me to elaborate (in explicit detail) what my memory of what happened was

1. I convinced myself that I indeed was
Gertrude Stein, and I was the last man on
Earth that believed in Earthly principles.
2. I went to where I felt the safest,
(Top of the Mark Hopkins)
3. I choose the pen and I choose the camera
4. Black Magic + White Magic = Rainbow Magic
Spirit of '77 that's my name. Animosity
+ Espionage = Good Film.

Or the story I wrote:

Children's Story
One day there was a tired old Math teacher who never spoke of life, love, or anything. He was a miserable math teacher. He often thought of all his illness, but he never remembered the good ole days when life itself was free of cost. He watched the Flintstones on TV and grew inspired. He went to Art School, but it was never any good, for him. For me, I thought about helicopters and the principles of keeping quiet. Writing for me was a good outlet. I was finally buried under a cloud of smoke. Thank you.

There is nothing else in there I can learn. I close the journal and walk to the TV room. I lost something but I'm getting it back. I look around the room at the people shuffling in their slippers and talking to themselves. I am one of them, but I'm getting better. I am not going to stay here. This is not my home. I am going home. I got accepted. I'm leaving. I get it back and they don't. I have something.

The medicine cart is here, and we all shuffle toward it in one big mass, like some weird outtake from Night of the Living Dead. I hate this place, but I won't tell anyone. I will keep quiet. I will behave and I will leave this place. I will drink my orange juice that stings the sides of my mouth and I will not say anything. I can feel a burn as the medicine goes down. Where is my pillow? I want my pillow, so I can hide my face from the nurses that will ask me what is wrong if they see my face. My bed is so far away, can I make it? I shuffle, as fast as possible, down the hallway and back to my bed. If they see my face I won't get that something back. They'll keep it from me and ask me questions until my head hurts and I cry for water. They won't let me go. I don't feel well at all. Are they taking it back from me right now? I'm in a movie. I'm in a cruel, dark, human movie. There is a narrator, and he's taking away my freedom. He's telling the audience what I'm going to do next. My pillow is here. It's not a feather pillow. It's filled with hypoallergenic spun plastic wool. The case is 80% polyester. It feels like I'm burying my face in a mop bucket, not a pillow. There is so little comfort here. I want to go home. I can't wait another fucking week.

"I can't wait a fucking week!" I scream it so loud my throat hurts. There are running footsteps in the hall, and they come into my room. I can't take my face out of the pillow. The scream was too loud.

"Ethan, what's going on?"

It's James, the fucking bastard head nurse that I'd like to kill. "Nothing."

"Why is your face in that pillow."

"I have a headache." There's a long pause. I think he's buying that one.

"Do you want a Cogentin?"

"Yeah, I'm sorta having a bad reaction to the Prolixin." Wow, that sounded really convincing, even I believe it.

"I'll get you a PRN right now. But you have to take your face out of that pillow, okay?"

"Okay, I will." I close my eyes as tightly as they will close. I close them so tightly that I see red behind the eyelids. Is that blood? Am I seeing blood in the blackness? I still haven't taken my head out of the pillow. James is waiting, he wants to see my face so he can ask me a thousand questions and keep me here for the rest of my life. Gently I lift my head and turn it toward him. I open my eyes, and there he is, with his hands on his hips. He's not nice.

"Are you going to write this down?"

"That's my job, Ethan."

"Please just say that it's a bad reaction to the medicine."

"I will. Did you have any reason to think I wouldn't? Is it something else that's bothering you?"

"No." Like I'd tell him. What would I say? 'Oh yeah, I was just thinking how much I'd like to kill you. I am pissed off at the narrator and I think you're in on his conspiracy.' Nope. I keep quiet and everything is fine. It's like a bad storm that passes through my consciousness, taking little brain cells and connecting them in bad ways and leaving things in a state of disorder. That would be a good thing to tell James. No. I'll keep quiet. James turns on his heels and saunters out to the medicine cart. He comes back with my Cogentin and a tiny glass of water.

"Do they save money by giving us smaller cups?"

"I don't know why they use such small cups. That's a good question, Ethan."

I think that's the first time he's said that I did anything good. I'll leave it at that. "Thank you for the PRN."

"No problem. I have to go write it up now."

"Bye." He's gone. Thank the Lord.

CHAPTER 18

They said I have to wait another week, because my medicine is reacting badly and they want to stabilize me on a lower dose. I hope it's not like college, where they give away your spot if you defer, like it says in the letter I got in the mail yesterday.

> Columbia College of Columbia University in the City of
> New York
> Office of the Dean
> July 31
>
> Dear Mr. Lloyd,
> It has come to our attention that during your leave of absence from our University you have become ill. Our wishes go out to you for a speedy recovery. It is the policy of Columbia University that a student who succumbs to an illness of your nature while on leave of absence must present a certificate of good health in order to return. The terms of your leave were for one semester only, and if you wish to return, we require a written request for extension. Barring receipt of those two items, we will be forced to give your spot to another incoming student. You may always reapply to our University in the future. I sincerely hope that California is working out well for you. Once again, get well soon.

Sincerely,
Lauren Crane
Dean of Studies

Fuck them. I hated it there anyway. I'm glad I have my journal with me. There are some good passages in here that remind me of how much I suffered there. Here's one that I wrote last year:

September 16

Another all-nighter. It's sad that I still can't love and I want to and the only thing that's changed is the seriousness of my situation. If I get too depressed, I'll just hop on a train and kiss this shit goodbye. I am still not in love. I've never been kissed, but I've done XTC and coke. There's a whole bevy of intriguing male specimens at Columbia, all of whom recognize me for the insane outcast that I am. They chortle at me. I wish I were a football player, hard and impenetrable. My tender soul has an instinct of its own which tells me to bug out of here. I'm going to get hurt too much in this inhumane institution of the humanities. HIGHER LEARNING IS FOR THE BIRDS. I'm insane. I can't fit into my pre-programmed place in society. I have been "prepped" for this experience and I call it SHIT. PURE BULL-FUCKING-SHIT.

I definitely wasn't happy there. So fuck you, Dean Crane.

*

I feel much better on my lower dose of Prolixin. I ran around the hospital today talking to everyone and feeling much more like my usual self. I rode imaginary skateboards with Jimmy for almost an hour before the staff stopped us. They made me clean up the places on the wall where my shoes left scuff marks. Jimmy helped. Sue came to visit, and we laughed and I said I was sorry for kissing her. She said that's okay, as long as I do it again. So I did. I felt much better about the second kiss. I think I do love her. But she's not a man. I guess we can work that out later.

Barbara says not to worry, because Northeast Lodge has accepted me and once you're accepted there they hold your spot. I want to see Northeast Lodge. Barbara says that it can be arranged! She calls up David and he tells her that he would like to see me and maybe interview me again at the Lodge. It's all happening so fast. Barbara has two taxi vouchers for me, and she tells me the address, 272 9th Street. She writes it on a piece of paper for me. I haven't been outside since the day the cop knocked me to the ground. Barbara walks me out of the door, past the "No patients beyond this point" sign. She says that there's a taxi waiting downstairs for me, Luxor Cab. Why are they letting me go? Didn't I run last time? I don't feel like running now, so maybe they can tell that. There's the cab, right out front, just like she promised.

*

Out the window of the taxi I can see familiar sights going past. He goes past Martin de Porres, where I sometimes would get a free vegetarian meal. There's the Vats, the old brewery that became a music practice space. There's no fog today, and everything gleams. We're underneath the freeway, and then he turns up Tenth street. There's the DNA lounge, where I did crystal. It's good to be back in San Francisco. The outer limits of the universe were not as comfortable as all this. Northeast Lodge is only a block away from the Stud, just like David said. It's a three story building. The whole building is covered in bright murals. The taxi driver lets me off at the front door. There's a little doorbell with a speaker box. I press it. After a minute, still nothing happens. I start to panic. What if they aren't there today? Why isn't anybody answering the doorbell? I ring it again. This time, someone answers. The voice comes out of the little box.

"Who's there?"

"Ethan."

"Who? Oh wait, are you here to see David?" I think it's a woman talking. She has a gravelly voice, probably a smoker.

"I think so. Who are you?"

"I'm Connie. David is expecting you, come right up."

The door buzzes and I pull it open. The scene inside is a little grim. The hallway is greenly lit with fluorescent lights. There are a few people standing in the hallway. None of them look like they work here. They must be inmates. One woman has eyeglasses with little dots of nail polish (cherry red) painted in the center of each eye. She seems a little frantic as she walks right up to me, a bit too close for comfort.

"Who are you?"

"I'm Ethan."

"I'm Dixie. This is my house." She walks away again, talking quietly under her breath to herself. I don't know where to go. I can't find anybody who works here. I do recall that Connie said "come right up" and there is a stairwell, so I take the stairs up a flight. This looks more like the right place. There's a door at the end of the hall, the kind that opens top and bottom. The top half is open, and there's a man in a white lab coat leaning out over the little counter.

"Hi, may I help you?"

"I spoke to Connie."

"That's me, love." I whirl around to see who said that. She has to be the coolest looking lady I've ever seen. Her hair is long and red, somewhat disheveled. A cigarette hangs out of her mouth. She wears a long black dress and a silver amulet around her neck. Her bony hands are covered in rings. There are wrinkles in her face deeper than a river. She smiles, revealing a yellowed row of oversized teeth. I think she and I will be friends. "David is expecting you. Come with me." She reaches out a bony hand and I take it. She walks me up another flight of stairs. David is in his office, behind a messy desk.

"Come in, come in." He points to a chair in front of his desk. I don't want Connie to go, because I like her. She lets my hand go and heads back downstairs. David still looks very round. "What do you think of the Lodge so far?"

"It's nicer than the hospital."

"Ho ho. It certainly is." Even his laughter is round. "Now

tell me, how did you wind up at General?"

"I figured out where itt's att." I keep forgetting not to talk about that. He frowns at me a little.

"I see. You had no trouble finding Northeast Lodge did you?" He peers out over his spectacles at me.

"The cab brought me here."

"Of course. Did you know that your mother has been here to see me?"

"No." I am stunned.

"Yes, she came here to make sure the place would be good enough for you. Now, please keep this confidential, but I think your mother may be part of the problem."

"How so?"

"Well, you'll have to forgive me for being so frank, Ethan, but your mother is a raving bitch. I just don't think it's healthy for you to stay too close to her."

I have an unwritten rule that states that only I am allowed to call my mother a bitch. David senses the frown starting to build on my face.

"We can talk more about her when you get here. I will be your counselor. I don't usually take on clients, now that I am director, but in your case I have made an exception."

"May I have Connie instead?"

I think that hurt his feelings. "No. I will be your counselor." He takes off his glasses and polishes them with a lens tissue.

"Are you gay?" I figured I might as well know.

"Yes I am. I assume you are as well?"

"Yeah." It was nice how comfortable I felt admitting it to him. I think he'll be an okay counselor.

"The reason I suggested you come here, Ethan, was to work up a plan for you."

"A plan?"

"Yes. We'll write down some goals that you have, and figure out how Northeast Lodge can help you to realize those goals. Now, what are some goals that you have in mind?"

"I'd like to get out of the hospital."

"Short term, very short term. We'll put that down, but it will be moot when you get here. Perhaps we'll broaden it to getting out of the mental health system in general, hmmm?" He jots something down on a carbonless form in a manila folder with my name on it. "Okay, anything else? Would you like to go back to Columbia?"

"No, they're a bunch of fuckers."

Only the corner of his mouth betrays his displeasure with my choice of words. "Wouldn't you like to go back to college?" he peers inquisitively at me from over his spectacles.

"No. I'm too sick."

"Ah, but if you were all well again, would college be of interest to you?"

"Maybe. Not Columbia."

"Very well, I'll put it down as a maybe. Not Columbia." He writes some more in my folder. "Now, we also need to decide on a project for you. We have two projects at Northeast, the mural project and the deli project."

"What are you talking about?" I feel worried, like I'm missing some piece of common knowledge.

"During the day, we have two projects that you can work on. One of them is the deli project, where you work with other clients preparing the food in advance for the Sunday brunch. The other is the mural project, where you spend the day painting the walls of the building, like what you saw out front."

"That was painted by clients?"

"Yes. With some assistance."

"I could never paint like that."

"Sure you could. Would you like to learn?"

"No." I genuinely fear painting. How can I ever leave a mark on anything for everyone to judge?

"It sounds like the deli project for you, then." He writes some more in my chart.

I'm really worried that I won't be able to do it. It's all I can do to tie my shoes at this point. I can't cook.

"What if I can't do it?"

"Then you won't be alone." He smiles. "Lot's of people here can't do it."

"Don't they have to leave?"

"No."

"NO?" I think to myself how nice it would be if Columbia University had been managed a little more like deli project.

David clears his throat and shakes his head no. He wipes his glasses with a cloth and smiles at me. Once his glasses are polished he puts them back on his round face and he is very, very round. I start to trace circles on my legs with my fingers. David leans forward and sees what I'm doing. "Does the medication agree with you?"

I shake my head no.

"Would you like to make that another goal then? To get off the medication?"

"Yeah." I'm starting to like this place now.

*

In the cab home, I mean the cab back to the hospital, I think about my nice gay counselor. He made me feel a little better about the whole thing, really. What did he say, "Lot's of people here can't do it." So maybe they're not so different from the folks at General. A lot of us can't do it.

When I get back to the hospital, my mom is waiting there. I really don't want to see her. She has a gift for me. It's a tiger tail key chain. She says I'll need it when they give me a key to the house. "I know you're always losing things. It's really hard to lose a tiger tail." She's always talking spiritual mumbo jumbo like that. I tell her I'm tired, but she's here to see me. In the smoking room there's some papers and some tobacco. She follows me in there while I roll a cigarette, or try to. She says I'm doing it wrong.

"Why don't you help me then."

"Because you shouldn't be smoking." It's hard to argue with her, she has a point.

"Well then maybe I'm doing it right." This makes her laugh

till tears roll from the corners of her eyes. I start to laugh too. It's been a long time since I laughed with her and it feels good. No one else can laugh like her, that way where her whole body shakes and you can't help but laugh just as hard. I can't roll my cigarette so I just put it down and keep laughing with her.

CHAPTER 19

Northeast Lodge took me in on a cold Monday morning in August. I bid farewell to all the inmates at the asylum and stuffed my belongings into a gym bag. There were so many gifts I had to put them in a bag all by themselves. Wanda's magic wand stuck out the top of the bag. Barbara the nurse saluted me farewell (no touching). Jimmy Simple wouldn't say goodbye to me, he just pouted in his room. I'll see him again so I said that I would and he just shrugged. I'd have hugged him but it would have gotten him into trouble. I was finally leaving the "space ship" on the alien planet and going back to San Francisco. The head nurse gave me one cab voucher and that means it's a one way trip. They don't want me back – and I don't want them back either.

*

Connie lets me in again at the front door. "Oh good, you're just in time for deli project." Oh shit, they want me in the kitchen. I can't I can't I can't. I start to panic but Connie just takes me by my hand (they allow touching here?) and gently drags me into the kitchen. I have all my stuff with me, and Connie says she'll take it up to my room. There in the kitchen is Gretchen Shoudt, the deli project manager. It takes very little time for me to realize that she is not a client, she's a counselor. She hands me a dull steak knife.

"Strawberries." She points to a giant stainless steel bowl full of strawberries. There must be twenty baskets worth. Next to it is another bowl, empty. "Do you know what to do?"

I shake my head no, dumbfounded.

Gretchen is about fifty years old, buxom and maternal. She has curly grey hair that escapes from her head in select places. Her face is very kind.

"I need you to take the tops off of all the strawberries and then cut them into little slivers, about yea big." She holds up a thumb and forefinger and rotates her wrist to indicate something about the size of a peanut. "Do you think you can handle that?"

Nervously, I start to tremble. It's been so long since I've had to do anything but arts and crafts. I am sure I used to cut strawberries, but never twenty baskets' worth. Gretchen has infinite patience. She takes me by the hand and leads me over to the cutting board. She takes a strawberry out of the bowl and places it on the board. She takes my hand and puts it on the strawberry. "Just use your fingers to hold it." With her other hand, she holds my steak knife hand and brings the knife in contact with the top of the strawberry. She applies pressure and I sever the strawberry from its leafy stem. "Good. Now chop that in two and throw it in this bowl." She indicates the empty stainless steel bowl beside the bowl of strawberries.

I throw the two small pieces of strawberry into the bowl. I notice that there is a lot of strawberry left on the stem that might need to be trimmed and thrown in with the other strawberries.

I hold the stem up so Gretchen can see the flagrant waste.

"Should I try to get more of the strawberry off of this?"

Gretchen smiles. "Nope. Trash it."

It only takes a few chops to remember all the time I spent in my mother's kitchen, dicing onions and bell peppers for burritos, or peeling potatoes to mash. I know how to cook. This medication makes me feel yucky, but I think I can cook in spite of it. I remember the time I didn't know how long to leave the refried beans on the stove. Mom said, "Just be sure they're hot enough to melt the cheese when we add it." That day, the burritos were perfect.

Then there was the time that Mom and I worked all day in the kitchen to prepare a Chinese feast. We hung marinated strips of beef off of curtain hooks and roasted them in the oven with a pan under them to catch the drippings. We made pot stickers and stir-fry vegetables. That was a lot of chopping that day. The pot stickers were completely from scratch, even the wrappers. We used a pot sticker mould that mom bought in Chinatown at the same time as she bought me my square-egg maker. It seemed like we had half the neighborhood over that day to eat Chinese food. Nobody went home hungry and we had Chinese leftovers for three days after.

Once in a while, Mom would let me make a dessert out of Maida Heatter's Book of Great Desserts. My favorite to make were the Mushroom Meringues. They were just egg whites and sugar whipped until they were stiff, and then put through a pastry tube to form little mounds and columns. I dusted them with cocoa and baked them in the oven. When they came out of the oven, they were solid little meringues. I melted Ghirardelli Dark chocolate and applied it to the underside of the mounds with a spoon. Then I quickly stuck the mound to the stem. When they were set, I would put them in a basket lined with a red napkin and set them in the middle of the table. Some of Mom's friends didn't even realize they weren't mushrooms until dessert time.

Gretchen stops by and exclaims, "You're nearly finished!" She's right. I don't really remember going through all of them. "I knew you could do it."

"Are you sure someone didn't help me?"

Gretchen shakes her head. "No. You did that all by yourself, Ethan."

*

Connie put my things on my bed. The room is dark, despite the fact that it has eastern exposure. The walls are musty landlord-white, with many stains and spots where the guests of this lodge have wiped their dirty hands or leaned their oily heads. The tattered curtains depict a colonial scene of pilgrims hoeing corn in the Fall. Out the window, the northbound traffic roars its way into the Tenderloin. I like it here.

I share the room with a short Chinese man with some kind of obsessive-compulsive disorder. He arranges and rearranges his comb, brush and other vanity articles in a rough clatter. After each arranging session, he looks up and waves. "Hello. I put my things away now, okay?" And then he starts to rearrange them again. This goes on most of the afternoon.

At 6 pm, Connie's voice comes over the loudspeaker. "Attention Northeast patients – it's med time." A familiar scene, but it's somewhat more civilized than the mad dash at the hospital. Everyone in the lodge lines up at a dutch door, patiently awaiting his or her meds. There's a lot of Chinese people here. Dixie, the girl with nail-polish dots on her glasses, is in line in front of me. She turns around to talk to me.

"How long have you been here?"

"Me? I just got here."

"Oh."

She turns back around for the moment. Carl, the Chinese man with the immaculate vanity dresser, talks quietly to himself in Chinese. Dixie reaches past me and taps Carl on the shoulder.

"Carl. Carl."

Carl stops his mumbling.

"Would you stop doing that? It's messing with my voices."

"Oh okay. Sorry." Then he goes back to mumbling, unaware perhaps that he is doing so. Dixie heaves a huge sigh of frustration and plugs her ears, singing a nonsense song. She has her back to the meds window and doesn't notice that it's her turn. Connie reaches out and taps her lightly on the shoulder. Dixie nearly hits her head on the ceiling as she jumps with astonishment.

"Jeez Connie! Don't scare me like that!"

Connie hands Dixie a paper cup with a small assortment of

pills. No orange juice here. It feels very grown up.

"Dixie honey, do you need a PRN of Ativan or anything?"

"No thanks, ma'am." Dixie dutifully swallows her pills and washes them down with Alhambra water. I step up to the window.

"Hi there, Ethan." It feels nice to be addressed by my name, especially from someone as cool as Connie. She hands me my cup, with its one little pill.

It's a tiny little pill. I stare at it for a second.

"Anything wrong?"

"No. I just haven't seen what it looks like before."

"Yeah, no orange juice here."

Now I know what it is I like about Connie; she gets what I'm saying. All those nurses in the hospital just dismissed me. The most common answer to anything I said was either 'oh, of course' or 'mmmhmmm-- nice.' Connie actually listens to me.

*

It's dinner time. The dinner is prepared by the clients. Everyone has kitchen duty twice a week. Tonight, it just so happens, is my night. I didn't know. Elliott, the kind avuncular client in charge of tonight's meal, tells me that I can do the dishes. I line up and eat with the rest of the clients. The meal is simple: baked hamburgers with tater tots and spinach. For dessert, it's ice cream and coffee. The hamburgers stick to the pans as Elliott dishes them out. It's going to take a long time to clean that up.

The spinach is stuck to the sides of the pot, too. As soon as I finish my hamburger, I put my plate in the grey plastic tub and head to the kitchen to soak the pots and pans. I fill the sink with hot soapy water.

It reminds me of the first night my mother taught me to do the dishes. We added bright green Palmolive to the plastic tub in the sink and generated lots of bubbles by setting the switch on the rubber head to spray as we filled the tub with hot water. "As hot as you can stand it." You put the utensils in the bottom of the tub to soak, in case there's any caked-on stuff on them. You also take the stickiest pots and pans and fill them with pure hot water, and add a little dish soap. Don't use Comet, even if the television says to, because it's poisonous and you don't want that shit sitting in a pot that you have to cook in. You have to wash the glasses first, since they'll show the most grease if you wash them later on. Plates are next, because they stack better in the drainer if it's mostly empty. We stacked them in one neat row, all facing the same direction. Next come the bowls, because they don't have as much grease as the pots and pans. They are harder to stack, because they come in so many shapes and sizes. Then you test the pans. Don't use a finger, because the water is still too hot. Take a fork out of the soapy tub and see if the sticky burnt stuff comes off easily. If it does, wash it. If it doesn't, let it soak overnight and then try again with the next set of dishes. Don't forget the forks and spoons. They'll clean really easily now, because they have been soaking this whole time. It was the first time I ever did the dishes. "Did you like it,"? she asked.

"It was kinda fun."

"Good. That's your job from now on." It was a trick! From that day forward, I always had to do the dishes, no matter how much I didn't want to. When Mork and Mindy was on, I couldn't watch because I had to do the dishes. That's life, I guess.

Elliott comes into the kitchen. He helps me put away the clean dishes by drying them with a dish towel. That was not something my mother taught me to do. She said they get cleaner if you let them dry naturally. She was an expert on dishes.

"How do you like it here so far?" Elliott has small eyes and disheveled, curly grey hair. He wears tinted wire rimmed glasses that make his face look rounder than it already is.

"It's okay, I guess."

"Yes. It's okay. It's better than the alternative."

I stop to ponder what that might be. The dishes are done. It's time for Coffee Walk.

I'm not clear what Coffee Walk entails. Elliott tells me to relax; it's the easiest activity going. He's in charge of the money. Everyone in the lodge treks out together, en masse, two blocks over to Café Soma. There are about twenty of us in all, descending on the staff who expect us. They roll their eyes and whisper among themselves. I can guess what they're saying. One of them notices me. "You're new."

I blush bright red. I want to say that I'm not with these people, and then I realize that I am. I really am with them. It's the first time I've stopped to feel ashamed of what happened to me. I don't say anything. I don't like coffee, either, so I don't have any. Dixie asks if she can have my share of the money to buy carrot cake.

CHAPTER 20

Later that night, Dixie adjusts her glasses so that the dots of nail polish align with her pupils. She saunters up the stairs to the landing, where smiling is allowed. I sit there, smiling and puffing on a More. In her fist she clutches an issue of Cosmopolitan. She turns to page 79. She has circled the number 79 many times using red ink, and the page is dog-eared.

"Ethan, I want you to see a picture of my daughter."

There was a picture of Naomi Campbell. Now Dixie is only about 30 years old and as white as they come, but she doesn't feel she has to explain that part. She turns to page 117, another daughter. It is a Guess Jeans ad with Claudia Schiffer.

"I'm so proud of my daughters. Aren't they wonderful?" She is utterly convinced. There is no use arguing, so I nod in agreement, suppressing a small smile. Dixie sees the smile and starts to chuckle. She turns to page 212, the Cosmo Quiz "Are You Man Enough to be His Woman?"

"Another daughter of mine, born in Kansas, wrote this."

"Your whole family is just all over this magazine, Dixie. You'd think you were the editor."

"Oh, I am. It's shameful nepotism, don't you think"?

We laugh aloud until tears stream down our face. Pretty soon, the whole lodge is up on the landing with us, smoking and laughing. I realize that I haven't laughed like that even once in the mental health system.

Dixie dances around on the landing and blows smoke rings. Elliott chuckles and tells her that she is a beautiful dancer. Suddenly, Dixie stops and whirls around to face him. Her face is twisted into a deadly serious grimace.

"Don't you objectify me. That's my business. I edit this magazine and I objectify women, not you!"

Elliott shrugs, unfazed. He just keeps laughing and pretty soon Dixie's angry personality subsides, replaced again by gales of laughter. She puts out her cigarette and turns to the inside back cover of Cosmo. It is the Virginia Slims ad: "You've come a long way, baby."

Pointing, she asks me "Do you recognize me?"

"Spit and image."

CHAPTER 21

Days roll by, followed by weeks. Dixie is going to be transferred, and she has a single room with its own toilet. I don't want to share my space with Carl anymore. He's too busy rearranging things to care that I am moving. I'm glad he doesn't take offense. They tell me I can have Dixie's room if I clean it after she leaves. Someone will come along to take her place at the Lodge, but I can have her room.

I give Dixie a hug goodbye, and she bumps her head on mine. "Take care of all your daughters, Dixie."

"They don't need my help, they're fucking millionaires."

"True. How true."

Dixie was going to a board and care home. They tell me it's where you go when you're not getting better. It's like day care for adults, but they outsource the day care at places called "Day Treatment Centers." David my counselor recently told me that I had to go to day treatment as part of my ongoing plan for recovery.

*

Central City Day Treatment is on Hyde Street. It's a tile covered building, with lots of crazy people inside. The people inside are not all crazy in the same way. Some are schizophrenic (like me) and some are Bipolar. Some are autistic and some are severely depressed. It's not a good idea to make crazy people peers with one another, because it's that much harder to figure out what's real when your neighbor is deluded too. A typical conversation at Central City Day Treatment might go like this:

> Client 1: Stop looking at my hair
> Client 2: It's a hair and a tortoise
> Client 3: Why do you keep taking and taking and never give?
> Client 2: Who asked you? Who made you president?
> Client 1: Yes, you are.
> Client 3: Where is the store?
> Client 1: Hair is good.
> Client 2: I saw your hair kill my baby.

It's in this Absurdist setting that I am expected to get well. It may mean that I am a snob, but I just don't want to be one of these people. It's like the feeling I get during Coffee Walk. I want to be cool again, like I was when I was friends with Donny. I want long black hair again. I want black fingernail polish. I want my zebra striped tights.

Wanda and Sue think I'm cool. They don't care what I look like. But they're in their late twenties, so they're older and more mature about this kind of thing. Kids my age, the cool ones, are going to take one look at me and think I'm a normie. They won't know that I used to hang out at the Underground, that I was the coolest looking person there besides Donny. They won't know. They won't know that I did a bunch of cool drugs.

The people who work at Central City Day Treatment do not understand me at all. Connie gets me, but these folks just do that hospital thing. They nod, and say things like "I imagine that must be pretty scary," or "I'm sorry you feel that way," or the worst one of all, "Mmmhmm...huh." It's time to apply to college.

*

Dixie's room is all clear when I get home from Day Treatment. The janitor actually cleared out her stuff for me. I come into the room and smile at my new space. Something isn't quite right. It smells weird. I open the window, which helps a little. There's nothing in the room. It smells like bathroom smell.

The toilet has not been flushed for several weeks. It's quite possible that Dixie was worried about what might happen if she did flush it. At first, her fears were unfounded, probably just a fear of the flushing noise. But now, no one can flush it. It's almost black and nearly overflowing. There's enough toilet paper in there to explode a septic tank.

Connie isn't on duty today; it's some other counselor. I tell her about Dixie's toilet. She says that we'll have to bring it up in house meeting tomorrow. That doesn't sound like a satisfactory answer and I tell her so. She says that the janitor isn't going to clean it. If I want the room, I'm going to have to clean it myself. She shows me where the cleaning supplies are. There's a bucket,

CHAPTER 22

Today I wake up very early and the feeling is back. It's not like I want to feel this way, but I just do. I try to shake off the feeling, but it's still there. I look at the table beside my desk and there's a pencil lying on the table that I DIDN'T PUT THERE. How did the pencil get there? It is not my pencil. I'm afraid to touch it. It's not my pencil. The pencil is from a hotel. It's from the Mark Hopkins Hotel. I didn't put it there. Why is it doing this to me? I need to get away from the pencil.

Out in the hallway, the few people who are awake this early ignore me. None of them can tell what I'm thinking, can they? They're not going to hurt me are they? I'm supposed to go to college today but I hate college because I can't read the Xeroxes and if I don't go to college then I have to go to day treatment but I don't want to. I hate day treatment. How can I get away from the pencil? The pencil is drawing a fence to keep me in.

A plan, a glorious, half-baked but delicious plan to escape the ill-placed pencil has hatched. Escape. Now.

In the kitchen, I pack enough supplies to keep me alive for a week. I stuff my backpack full of granola bars, apples, string cheese, dried apricots, anything that will survive outside a refrigerator. I take two liters of water from under the counter. I will never see that pencil again.

Outside, there are aliens. I see them at the bus stop, one eye looking up toward heaven, one eye piercing my very soul. They are the good aliens, but they can see right into me and they want to control me. I need to get away. I know what I need to do. The aliens are beckoning me. I climb on board the 27 bus line (that's the day of my birthday) and everyone on the bus is an alien. All the eyes are wall-eyed. With my crazy card, the fare is only 15 cents. I pay it and stand, because all the seats are filled with aliens.

The bus drops me at the Powell Street BART Station. It's exactly where I belong. How did they know I belong here? This is the only BART station where I can buy the crazy card BART ticket. They're red, not blue, and they cost 10 cents on the dollar. I buy a 10 dollar ticket for 1 dollar. I wait for a train. It can be any train. A Richmond train pulls into the station. On board, there are a few helper aliens watching me, protecting me.

I get off the train in a familiar place. I take the steps two at a time, knowing that I have a deadline. I turn left and head for the same spot. There stands the same black man who discouraged me and Donny from catching the night train all those months ago. He smiles, one eye staring toward heaven, one eye piercing my soul. He nods, and a train comes around the bend at a crawl. Three miles per hour tops. The train comes between me and the man, and as I look between the cars, I can see him smiling at me, and then he vanishes. The next car is an empty box car, doors wide open. It's mine. I don't know if it's going to LA or Seattle or Chicago or Mexico City, but this car is mine.

Acknowledgements

There are hundreds of people that deserve thanks and praise for helping me to reach the place where I could write this book. God, or the almighty, or Allah or whatever you choose to call it, was the single most powerful force that influenced my ability to heal and tell my tale. The doctors and nurses of Ward 6B General hospital were also instrumental. The counselors, staff and patients at Northeast Lodge, Conard House, and the Haight Ashbury Free Drug Clinic were also a major part of my healing experience. Guiding me out of adolescence and into adulthood were my family and friends. I will try to list them by name, at the risk of leaving out a few: Maggie Dusheke, Allan MacLeod, Jacqueline MacLeod, Sheila Peatfield, Kim Davis, Greg Douthwaite, Brenda Knight, Liane Angus, Saida Benson, Lenore Feyleaves, David Bineault, Robert X, John Yates, Lillian Crist, Jimmy McNally, Claudia Gonson, Stephin Merritt, Billy Hernandez, Barry Barbour, Joan Schurr, Catherine Enderton, Eric Enderton, Herbert Enderton Sr. and Jr., Joe Mama, Michael G. Page, Sistar Aquadivina, Cosmos Bell, Tom Gulager, Lisa Cardone, John Gulager, Clu Gulager, Miriam Gulager, Diane Ayala Goldner, James Claffey, Willow Garner, Lance Chau, Rebecca Wetherby, Tobias Fifield, Norman Gholson, Kevin Burke, Amedeo Pignatelli, AronNora Morgan, Marie Barr, Jan Jurgens, Amelia Antonucci, Timothy Doyle, and Lynn Cursaro. Helping me to craft this book: Sonia Morin, Michele Seipp, Wayne DeSelle, Guia Avesani, Mark Harvey, and the many other writers with whom I shared earlier versions of this book. Rafael Navarro, my partner, has stood by my side and cared for me through thick and thin, and for that, I will be eternally grateful. To all of you, thank you for putting up with my occasional *locuras* and for helping to steer me towards lasting sanity!